A NOVEL ›››››››››››››››››››››››››

BABYLON

›››››››››››››››››RENÉ CREVEL

Illustrated by MAX ERNST

Translated and with an
Afterword by KAY BOYLE

North Point Press San Francisco
1985

Originally published in French as *Babylone*, 1927;
translation published by arrangement with
Éditions Jean-Jacques Pauvert, Paris.
Translation and Afterword copyright © 1985
by Kay Boyle.
Chapter one, "Mr. Knife, Miss Fork," was
originally published by Black Sun Press in a
limited edition in 1931.
Max Ernst's photograms are printed with
the permission of Dallas Ernst.
Printed in the United States of America.
Library of Congress Catalogue Card Number: 84–62302
ISBN: 0–86547–191–6

Preface

René Crevel, essayist and novelist but essentially poet in everything he wrote, was born with our century and chose to live only half the allotted biblical human time. A student of eighteenth-century rationalism, he was engaged in writing a treatise on Diderot when he encountered the surrealists and, joining this group of iconoclasts, came to believe that Reason had betrayed the mind. Seizing upon the philosophical implications of surrealism, he transferred broad spiritual questions to a twentieth-century form of materialistic dynamism. His *poesis* became manifest in a vibrant, anguished, sometimes mocking prose and in the unconventional way of life he chose, much of it engaged in intense dialogue with the members of the surrealist community, particularly under the tutelage of André Breton. While the surrealists talked of rebellion, Crevel embodied rebellion. Fellow surrealist Philippe Soupault said of him: "He was born a rebel the way others are born with blue eyes." And when in 1935 the Congress of Writers in Defense of Culture, meeting in Paris under strong Stalinist leadership, impeded the liberty of speech of the surrealists, Crevel chose self-immolation as his ultimate surrealist act of protest.

René Crevel's substantial work of some ten volumes became lost to readers of his own generation and only reemerged in print in France some forty years after his death. It is, therefore, as much out of context today as was Rimbaud's famous message contained in a letter written in 1871 but not made public until 1912: that poetry is a search for knowledge and not mere self-expression. So, in the faithful translation of his hypnotic *Babylone*, Kay Boyle can present René Crevel to the American public as a living contemporary. Unburdened by critical references, Crevel reaches his readers as a fruit ripened on the tree, to be savored in all its freshness in his "fanfare of sobs"* as he confronts the cosmic forces and human phlegmatism in relation to them.

ANNA BALAKIAN

*Etes-vous fou? (Paris: Gallimard, 1929), p. 33.

BABYLON

Mr. Knife,
Miss Fork

A little girl asked, "What is death?" but without leaving time for a response forestalled any by saying: "And since you believe everybody dies, don't try to make me believe it's the same thing as being asleep. People who are having a good time are never sleepy . . ."

The mother was of a family that drank only water, suspected the effects of pepper, banished Worcestershire sauce from the table, as well as pickles and even mustard, but willingly held forth between the fruit and cheese upon the question of social hygiene. On the threshold of her thirtieth year, this mother was already resigned to the dreariest and most useless of virtues.

"It is all very well," she stated, "for those who are having a good time never to be sleepy, but they'll die like all the others.

No man can escape that fatal law for, my child, death . . . death
. . ."

"Oh, yes, I know. Death is something like Cousin Cynthia. Even before I knew Cynthia I thought of nothing but her. Besides, at the house, at every meal everyone talked about her. They could hardly wait to see her, and Grandma kept saying: 'Cynthia will be our ray of sunshine.' What joy the day she arrived! She brought such nice presents for everyone, and with her red hair, her green dress, and her eyes gray like clouds, you knew right away she was born in a country that you, you'll never go to. We put her in the prettiest bedroom, and she could have stayed there for years and years, but one fine day, no more Cynthia. She ran off without saying anything. Like a robber. And when she left, she took Papa with her. At first I thought it was a joke, but they didn't come back. Grandma, like always, played the proud lady, and said we mustn't be sorry they were gone, and the only thing to do was to let them gad about wherever they wished. But Grandpa, he has it in for Cynthia especially. He calls her the funniest names, and the other night he shouted out loud that she was a whore. A whore, what is a whore? And tell me, is death a whore too?"

Silence.

She who was asked these questions closed her lips as tightly as she could, as if she feared she might, in surprise, let slip a word, a phrase. But childish curiosity does not so easily give in, and a look was thrust straight into the woman's eyes, as if by pressing there it could force to spring out of the muteness the secret kernel of sound.

"What is death? What is a whore?"

A little voice tirelessly repeated the question, and to the

mother's surprise that burrowing mole, uncertainty, began hollowing its tunnels.

Deprived by atavism of the pagan possibilities of joy, this faded blonde, abandoned prematurely as she was, made no attempt to free herself of the memory of her domestic failure by twisting facts around. Her husband had left for an unknown destination, and as naturally as she had given nine months of her life so that her body might bring forth another body, so did she determine to devote the years that were to come to the spiritual formation of the fruit of her womb. Moreover, her own candid and materialistic father, a bearded psychiatrist, asked nothing better than to aid her with the gifts of his mind.

On this particular day he was, unfortunately, out of town. True, quite recently when questioned upon the subject of an early sexual education, he had so stressed the complexity of the question that our sequestered Maintenon was utterly at a loss, once he was done, to know what to believe. But who would dare ask the great man to clarify the matter further, this man whose indulgence for the human race, its instincts, its vices, and its follies, was measured with such disconcerting precision? Besides, his titles, his assurance, and his world renown intimidated those of his own flesh and blood as much as they were flattered by them.

But once the little girl had asked again, "What is death? What is a whore?", there was no longer the need of advice from a specialist in psychology to persuade the mother that it was wiser to postpone a bit longer the perilous task of explaining the mysteries of procreation. In the meantime, it was impossible not to be upset by such curiosity. At this child's age, the mother would never have had the audacity to ask such questions, and, moreover, could not even have imagined them. And certainly the hunger to know, the thirst for experiment, however imperative they might be in the family, were not enough to explain this insistence. How, furthermore, could a mind even in its extreme youth submissive to facts not feel shame for the word that had escaped the lips in a moment of anger, lips that, after all, could not make use of colorless epithets to describe a redheaded jade who had emerged from the fogs of her native land for the sole purpose of stealing from the most faithful of wives a husband whom virtue could no longer hold?

In fact, here we are. The child's absurd imagination came from the faithless one. A strange race, that race of little girls whose fathers have taken leave of the continents of wisdom for creatures with hair of flame. That the young father in question had neither principles, nor system, nor morals was eloquently proved by his conduct. It remained to be seen if the little girl would choose the vagabond frivolity of one of her generators or the austere submission of the other. That she had spontaneously seized on the role played in her parents' disunion by a brazenly painted woman bore witness to her remarkable sense of intuition, no less than to a precocity of rather bad agio. And how was it possible not to deplore her penchant for the bizarre? Indeed, the interest that she had in her fatal cousin was not the only symptom of its kind, and the mother now recalled a whole series of blue men, of violet houses with orange roofs, of red fields, and various other improbabilities messed out of the child's first box of watercolors.

Useless to point out that there is a white race, a yellow, a black, a red, but none the color of the sky; or that houses are built of stone or brick and are white or rose, or that grass in the fields grows green. A child reconstructs the world according to his own caprice, preferring above all the fabulous animals, making fun of the swans in the Bois de Boulogne, laughing in the faces of the bears in the Jardin des Plantes, despising lions, camels, elephants, and deigning to look with a less severe eye on the rhinoceros, thanks to the horn that is planted on him where there was no reason to expect to find one. And how many questions were asked about the gnu that the old cook, last autumn in the country, used to chase away at dusk?

At the moment, the apocalyptic beast is death, and again, with eyes big enough to swallow the whole universe:

"What is death? What is a whore?"

"The lesson is over, my darling."

"But you haven't answered."

"Go and play. Tell your nurse to give you your tea."

The child saw it was useless to persist. She went straight to the pantry, but not to ask for bread and butter. She took a knife, a fork, and quickly hid in a corner of her room, and, very softly, for herself alone to hear, began saying:

"The knife is Papa. The white part that cuts is his shirt; the black part you hold in your hand is his trousers. If the white part that cuts was the same as the black part, I could say he was in pajamas, but it's too bad there's no way to do that.

"The fork is Cynthia. Beautiful Cynthia, the English lady. The part you stick into the things you want to take off your plate, that's Cynthia's hair. She has a pretty bosom that moves up and down because she is out of breath. Papa is very happy. He caresses Cynthia, and he laughs because he thinks it is two little birds she has closed up in her dress, so he makes a declaration to her:

" 'You know, Cynthia, I love you. I am in love with you. When we go down hallways, I am always mad to kiss you. You

are so beautiful with your red hair and your green dress. I want my little girl later on to look like you. Handsome young men will come to court her and she will marry the one who plays tennis the best. My wife, she knew a lot of things. Of course, she was as well educated as you, but you couldn't have a good time with her very often. Now us, when there's just the two of us, we laugh and sing. Now we're going to take a trip. Every night we'll have a new room, but always with the twin beds as close as possible to each other, and we'll talk a long time before going to sleep. We'll stay in bed late every morning. We'll eat in dining cars, and so that nobody will recognize us I'll call you Miss Fork. You, you'll call me Mr. Knife, and people will think we're a Spanish couple on our honeymoon. We'll go to very gay places where there will be flowers as soft as your hair, and in shops I'll buy you beautiful dresses with very low necks. In hot countries we'll drink lemonade so cold and prickly that it will make us sneeze. At the North Pole, before going to bed, we'll put so much rum in our tea that we'll laugh ourselves to sleep. We'll climb all the Eiffel Towers. If we run into any tigers, I'll give you my arm and you won't be afraid. On the icebergs, we'll see seals playing ball with their noses and we'll bring one back to amuse us when we're old. We'll send hummingbirds and rhinoceros horns to my little girl. We'll also write to her on handsome postcards, for I think she must be very bored with her mother who gives her a lesson in arithmetic every day. We must be nice to her because we two are so happy together. I love you so much, Cynthia. You are not like other women. You are much more beautiful. You are like death, Cynthia, you are a whore like death, Cynthia, my darling, my little whore . . .' "

Several weeks later, at lunch, the child, seated between her grandfather and grandmother, asked why the fourth chair was empty, her mother's usual place.

"Your mother wasn't feeling well this morning, but she's coming down right away."

And, indeed, a few minutes later the door opened, and in came the young woman, eyes red in a gray face. She sat there sniffling, unable to swallow a mouthful. The grandmother shrugged her shoulders, persisting in the rhythm of contempt that served as metronome for her entire existence. The grandfather, his beard more majestic than ever, fork in one hand, knife in the other, like complementary scepters of Justice and Authority, searched for a phrase that would encompass the situation, while the child could not help thinking:

"I only hope he won't see that the knife is Papa and the fork Cynthia. They certainly would have a bad quarter of an hour, poor things . . ."

But hardly had the child time to formulate this fear within herself than already the *paterfamilias* had begun to speak in the beautiful, grave voice that gave such a troubling appearance of depth to the least of the diagnoses or announcements he might make at the Academy of Medicine.

"Your husband, a gangrened limb, nothing can be done to save it. Sooner or later one would have had to consider amputation, otherwise . . . otherwise . . ."

A gesture of his hands opened the field to the most terrible suppositions. And to continue:

"The wisdom of nations is sound when it declares 'birds of a feather flock together.' The redhead will not let him get away that soon. Undoubtedly our mistake was to take that girl into our midst, but if it had not been that one, he would have gone off with another . . ."

Then, hearing her irremediable misfortune confirmed, the abandoned woman let her emotion spill down over her beef-steak and potatoes. Great debacle. She chewed up her sorrow with her meat, and swallowed with gurgles of despair a meal watered with tears, while the psychiatric patriarch continued:

"I know, I know you are emotional. You take after your dear mother. I am the first, however, to recognize that it is at least enough to bowl one over. The scandal is not restricted to one capital. A London paper is now publishing the photographs of the runaways and already announcing their marriage, even though your divorce hasn't yet been granted . . ."

The grandmother, not having seen the document in question, asked that it be fetched for her, so here was the child sent off to find the English daily on the first page of which, printed between the photograph of a Whitechapel satyr a few minutes before he was hung and a bride medieval to excess coming out of Westminster on the arm of a young, immaculate, and smiling lord, was a Cynthia dripping with pearls, so perfect as to throat and face that, in spite of the poor quality of the paper and ink, her brow, her cheeks, her shoulders, and her arms seemed polished by a sunlight of joy, as iridescent as if a rainbow were breaking in triple cascades of brilliance over her skin, her dress. One wrist was so weighted with bracelets that the hand, like a drenched bird in April sunlight, rested momentarily on the arm of a chair, while the other, barren of rings, bathed in the foam of pearls that cascaded from the silky summit of her breasts. The foam of pearls became a lake in that fragile plateau that the dress of a seated woman hollows between her knees. In a little rectangle cut out of the miracle of her skirt was the head of the young father who had allowed himself to be bewitched. Below, three lines to say that he was the son-in-law of the most celebrated European psychiatrist, and to explain the adventure, to give a few names.

The child knew they were waiting for her, and that she could not stay hours in contemplation. For one last second, she looked at Cynthia with all her strength, then closed her eyelids so that with a darkroom of memory, no new image would spoil by superposition the photograph of the marvelous photograph of Cynthia.

On tiptoe, she groped her way back to the dining room where the family was too occupied with the portrait to notice that her eyes were closed. But if she was unable to see her grandmother study through her lorgnette this piece of evidence as gravely as the bacteriologists of the family examined germs under their microscopes, she at least heard the judgment pronounced:

"My poor sister, she would be better dead than see her jade of a daughter photographed half-naked under her pounds of false pearls. Her dress, have you noticed Cynthia's dress? You'd think she was decked out for the Martinique sun instead of for the fogs of England, the last country of Europe, however, my dear brother-in-law used to say (the unfortunate father of this creature), where a certain notion of dignity is preserved. At any rate, our young slut won't die of the heat, with her three rags around her hips. And to think we took in and lodged such a Messaline! When I think of my sister, so upright, so well balanced! She was very young when she left us to marry a colleague of Father's in London. But even abroad she conducted herself as admirably as she had in France, and never did she fail to measure up to our traditions. Of course, my brother-in-law, in spite of the difference in race, was really one of our own sort. I can see him now, immaculate, economical (a little more in that direction and he might have been judged a skinflint). What did he and his wife, with their good hearts, ever do to have such a creature as a daughter? How stupid men are. Think, my dear child, the family life we offered your husband. We are not the kind to go in for a lot of high jinks. But all the same, people of note have never seemed to be too bored in our company. And even in offering a toast at the end of a banquet, some intern or other of your father's went so far the other day as to praise his dry wit . . ."

"Tra-la-la-la-la-la-la-la-la," the little girl sang to herself, not opening her eyes until she was sure the family had got up and left the room. Then, because the fruit looked so sad in its colorless bowl, she dreamed of the delight of eating ice cream, happily seated on a red plush bench between Cynthia and her father, while an orchestra harmonized the flowers strewn on the tablecloth with its notes and chords and with a joy that disdained words. Dear Mr. Knife, dear Miss Fork!

"You know, Papa, you know, Cynthia, if Grandma says bad things about you it's because she's mad. She'd love to have bracelets and necklaces herself, for she knows perfectly well that she's not pretty with her wrinkled skin, her ugly black dresses, and her old fur-piece that smells like a wet dog, and her crazy hat on top of her head. I don't answer when she fusses at me, but just wait until the day I'm grown up and see if I stay home and play cards or do my scales after dinner! Every evening I'll put on a new dress with a very low neck and flowers on my shoulder. I'll have gold slippers and a pink feather fan as big as me. Then I could become an actress. I'll sing songs that don't mean anything, and I'll laugh and I'll dance like the American lady we saw this summer at Vichy, at the casino. They'll bring me bunches of flowers the way they did to the

American lady, and I'll come back five or six times for the applause. When I leave, young men will fight to get me to go in their cars. I'll always pick out a red car because it's prettier in the country, and if you go very fast you can kill chickens or even sheep on the road without it leaving any mark. When Cynthia came, Grandma wasn't jealous yet, and she kept repeating all day: 'My sister's daughter is a beauty with her crown of flames.' That's the truth. Cynthia's hair is so beautiful that you'd think you'd burn your fingers if you dared to touch it. Papa must be proud to live with such a beautiful lady who has such pretty color on her cheeks. A man can't be happy if his wife looks ill. But there it is: Grandpa and Mama will never understand. Today Papa is wearing white flannel trousers, because this is a knife with an ivory handle. He is at the seashore. The tablecloth is the Atlantic Ocean. Cynthia is climbing a rock. Papa wants to follow her. He slips because of the seaweed. Cynthia catches hold of him and saves him from falling in the water. He thanks her, kisses her hand, not the end of her fingers, but the inside where it is always so soft . . .

"Then he says: 'Cynthia, you have just saved my life. You are so light and slender, but even when you climb on a rock in the middle of the ocean you are quite at home. If I didn't know who you were and I saw your picture in the paper, and also a picture of some murderer, I'd hardly be able to wait to read all about Cynthia. I wouldn't even look at the story about the murderer because there is something so wonderful in *you*.'

"The lovers hold each other very tight because here it is evening, and it's cold. All of a sudden, it is night. A big bird comes and sits on Cynthia's head. He likes her hair better than his own nest."

★

★   ★

In the fog of dreams, the name of Cynthia caught fire every night. Not a meal passed without vituperation of the adventuress, the redhead. The professor with his big beard asserted (without being asked) that work is still the best remedy for melancholic obsession, and, so that the abandoned woman might forget her misery, he asked her to aid him in his research. Thus, when there were guests at dinner, the psychiatrist drew himself up with dignity and referred to her as "my collaborator," or as "the most gifted of my students," or something of that ilk.

As for the fugitive father, kingpin of this painful clearing of the decks, as the familiar saying goes, they saw him only once, when he was obliged to pass through Paris for the divorce proceedings. The child had intended to ask him a thousand questions about Cynthia, her pearls, her dresses, their trip, their happiness. But from the monologues of the day and the dreams of the night such high, and also such preemptive, phantoms had come into being that she could not risk their confrontation with daily possibilities. So in proud discretion, she did not breathe a word of all that had been hours on hours of delight and torture to her, thus condemning herself to remorse for never having revealed either her affection or her confidence to the pale young man whom she continued to call father, but who must now ring the doorbell of an apartment to which he once had the keys, and where today his sudden presence made an empty space.

A winter, a spring, Cynthia remained a flaming idol in her memory, in turn brightening the gray heavens or warming the finical azure of the minutes to the color of a painting between two showers. But after the blazing passage of the young woman with a helmet of fire across that azure, the little girl, her eyes still dazzled by the miracle, could not repudiate that beautiful comet. Then came the nauseatingly pious anecdotes by which the family glutted its hate . . .

Cynthia, redheaded goddess, from your fingers sprang arrows of light, but once flown they only heightened the sorrow of days that followed, all of them alike. Boredom, the stepson of pride: the repetition of facts and gestures, the collection of untruths by which those called "grown-ups" live, these one childhood had sworn never to accept.

She imagined mornings without lies, cloudless afternoons, weeks not filled with stupidities. Who then would dare refuse her, in exchange, the harsh right to judge a woman so without grace in life that she did not stop complaining about a man whom she would never see again? And the professor, all hair and spectacles, who repeated as often as possible that salvation lies in work, as if he had to keep saying it every instant so that he wouldn't stop being sure of it, and the old woman who raged because another had been preferred to her daughter. The child could not believe that people who have the right to walk the streets at any time of the day or night are interested in nothing and nobody except Cynthia and a son-in-law on whom they had perversely set limits of bad breeding and frivolity.

A winter, a spring. The hour strikes for the lighting of lamps. Instead of getting up and going to the electric switch, a little girl accepts the night, which sets no limits on childhood's rooms. Dreams without images, song without words, obscurity sweeps all the sordid dust away at last and opens a door upon unfathomable depths. Syllables only for her who pronounces them, hands on her knees, her voice low, syllables not weighted by meaning are murmured, sisters of the wind, while its invisible triumph casts a halo of transparent birds around all living creatures, victorious over the fury of the seas, over the cries of the creatures; a sudden whirlpool is at the threshold of the Shakespearean forest where Cynthia, in the finest moment of her triumph, bestows enchantment far and wide. Then, weary of the banal talk of men, she disappears in complete mystery to the tune of a page boy singing:

With a hey and a ho and a hey nonino.

With a hey and a ho and a hey nonino. Cynthia and her pearls, her plumes, her miracles weighed no more than a verse from *As You Like It* in reveries at the end of the day. But all during dinner, alas, one had to resign oneself to the stupidly, uselessly concise language of men. Over their heads, having emerged from the soup tureen like "Venus from the Ocean," and as worthy of being the daughter of an ordinary soup as the most beautiful goddess of the elusive foam, the hanging lamp cast shadows like those of a ridiculous dancer, and from the skirts of this ballerina fell, in the guise of light, a miserable green.

Then, because far, very far away on the open plains of a night where no domestic fire burned, where no face brought to the family dinner table in the evening the tribute of its age, its weariness, its rancors, because, without bumping into objects or creatures the wind was going on its way, singing to live, living to sing, fearing nothing or no one, a child who refused to be caught up in small talk, small things, small people, closed her eyes, and as she swallowed the food before her without tasting it, at every beat of her heart she was aware of the indomitable murmuring:

With a hey and a ho and a hey nonino.

« CHAPTER TWO »

To Revive
the Wind

Summer.

The grandfather and the mother had to remain in Paris because of their work. The grandmother settled in with her granddaughter on the family property in the Seine-et-Oise.

Queen of a box-bordered garden, the old lady drenched her roses with a syringe, as if those persnickety creatures had need of a clyster to preserve the pretty color, the natural delicacy of flowers. The hour of the daily apotheosis rung, and the intricate task once performed (which for nothing on earth would she abandon to the uncouth indifference of mercenary hands), the grandmother ascended in great dignity the steps of the belvedere from where each car she perceived gave her a pretext for regretting the majestic and dustless era of victorias and princess gowns. But, despite the arrogance of the Hispanos and the im-

pertinence of the Citröens, she would remain faithful until
death to the beloved horizon that set limits with such artistry
to the hodgepodge of villas, kiosks, latticework, convoluted
trees, etc.

"What a magnificent lawn, what splendid flowerbeds, what
a pretty countryside!" she would exclaim in ecstasy.

A binocular played the role of scepter and pointed out the
marvels of the scenery. Above all, see the variety of this kingdom: here a Chinese verandah in faience, wrought iron, bronze,
and stained glass, created by a dealer in precious metals, a man
of good taste and means who had the idea of embellishing a
little eighteenth-century countryseat so simple, so bare that its
stones seemed almost immodest; there, on a flawless lawn, in
contrast to the apoplexy of the geraniums, was the anemic blue
of the hydrocephalic hydrangeas; then, a bit farther, an entire
regiment of porcelain turtles, watched over from the height of
a roof by a family of fabulous birds . . .

Paltry remnants of woods, of hills, what kind of ridiculous
sauce attempted to add spice to the pretensions of these sub-
urbanites. In the cement pools, goldfish revolved in such formation that one no longer recalled that others, humbly gray,
live in waters unimprisoned by paint-daubed grottoes, waters
that flow carefree through meadows where peaceful oxen
graze. But all the lords of these ridiculous parterres had never
known that fruit hangs innocently from trees before compro-
mising itself with cream in the dubious mystery of Neapolitan
ices.

The child preferred the Louis-Philippe salon (congealed
though it was in smug self-satisfaction) to the contorted pathways, the sophisticated lawns. At least she found there the ref-
uge of shade, a cool cube of air where she could forget the

flamboyant insult of day. Furniture with petticoated slipcovers, secret closets, sofas eternally weary, resigned to an inglorious old age, your slightly musty sweetness gave her confidence. Why go out when from the threshold there came a heavy odor of work and servitude, under the hot canvas of an awning where the clumsy acrobat of fire had fallen, as at the circus the one in pink tights falls into the net?

Bondage of the soil and of the plants. A gardener with sleeves rolled up, an old lady in gardening gloves, syringe in one hand, pruning shears in the other, persecuted this soil, these plants, one with brutality, the other with the petty meannesses of a hypocritical nurse. Only a few trees had succeeded in preserving a little of their freedom, but they still did not know how to make use of it, since the poplars let their cotton fall in scrofulous negligence to the ground, and the linden trees scorned the gold hearts they rained down in full wheelbarrow loads in order to strengthen the fabric of their good intentions. One weeping willow flatly emulated the Andromache of classical matinées. As for the apple trees, twisted with rheumatism, what dreams in their branches could the protectors of childhood cling to? So, in the twilight of a house with curtains drawn, in the lap of an armchair of mahogany and velvet from Gênes, there was a solace, almost a joy, in learning better and better each day that there are weeks, months, years, that count for peanuts.

Reborn, then, the rusty fogs of winter; Cynthia, Cynthia, tawny reflection illuminating the premature nights, much more is needed than an actual sun in the actual heaven to dispel the miracle of your evanescent light. Warm minutes, becalmed hours, sea of oil, without promise of a sail on the horizon, blessed be the ray of memory that is at last about to pierce the immobility of the present with a surface that appears to be without transparency. The waves suddenly part, and unsuspecting ferns, in their lively arabesques, light the secret of the depths. At an equal distance between the surface and the bottom, a man (impeccable evening jacket), a woman (gown fluid, cape greenish-blue) float side by side. Driftwood without substance sustained by the most ethereal of breaths, the face of no earthly creature was ever lit by smiles as calm, as pure, as yours. But your hands, in spite of immobility, have kept that flexibility creatures lose with the breath of life. Phantoms, float impassively on among the waves of memory. On earth, the tide is low and the waters of time have ebbed far out. Those who have never ceased to actuate a mundane life are already at a loss as to what pretext to give themselves as goal. Summer noon, the hour has struck for renouncing those details that underscore the senselessness of familiar lights. In the shade of closed eyelids, to which aggressive banalities refuse the access of sight, but where, however, night cannot possibly remain, for even in concave velvet and silence, the triumphal fire springs to life.

The past a crampfish,* a gulf is ripped from bottom to top, and from the most inoffensive of foams suddenly darts a flash of lightning that the depths toss back to the sky. Thus, at twilight, the surroundings of graveyards are crowned with little flames (will-o'-the-wisps, frightened servant-girls call them when passing the dormitories of the dead)—phosphorus, the positivistic grandfather explained to his granddaughter, who decided:

"Phosphorus, but why not? Phosphorus is even prettier than Jerome, which could already easily be the name of a flower. Papa and Cynthia aren't Mr. Knife and Miss Fork any more.

*Translator's note: A crampfish is the same as an electric ray.

They're called Mr. and Mrs. Phosphorus, for now they're husband and wife, Mr. and Mrs. Phosphorus . . . Phosphorus . . . My phosphorus . . ."

Her phosphorus, it danced on the crest of her dreams. It went on, a couple united forever by the miracle of fire. Gentle swimmers of memory, float horizontally, and let nothing of human concern distress you. Flowers heavy on the stem of a neck wearied by the weight of pearls, and another whose immaculate prison of linen has not deprived it of its flexible grace, your faces are not hollowed by fear, nor painted with a false joy, nor tortured by hate, your faces, as perfect as ivory eggs, are crowned by a cortege of flamboyant fish. A fire of tortoise shell on the surface of the sea, an aurora borealis of mother-of-pearl as far as the inviolate pole, raises the two lovers up again. An armchair of mahogany and red velvet has become the hull of a vessel following their dazzling wake.

Phantom ship, submissive to the gentle ebb and flow of silence, your voyage, a miracle between heaven and earth, comes to an end when night falls on the ridiculous gardens. Then the child navigator knows it is better to come alongside habitual ground, to abandon the salon of afternoon, its wondrous gulfs, for the banal garden of men and its pathways, its lawns, which darkness will slowly restore.

Soon the old ladies will have left their terraces, followed by servants carrying the sewing tables, and the grandmother herself will have come in. No longer any need for her to make seven times the rounds of a prison, so that the walls that had opened wide to the unending smile of the waves—the opposite to those of the Biblical city—would reconstruct themselves, and with stones so inexorably joined that no Cynthia, no weightless ghost, would be able to slip through. Outside, the revenge

of darkness will have transformed a poplar into an aviary of songs, and, by the gentle grace of dusk, the pathways, the hopes of the hour, would be unlimited. The wind, the wind, at last . . .

The wind . . .

But the hour had not yet struck for its resurrection among the leaves. Suddenly a door banged, an easily recognizable voice yelped. Words like arrows, javelins of curt commands, let fly from the threshold were not sharp enough that evening to penetrate the torpor of the pantry. Feeling them blunted against the wall, a woman, whose intonation was at first as imperative as usual, was not long in losing her arrogance. One imagines her haggard, frantic with terror, and, indeed, she recovered sufficient strength and tone of voice only to cry out: "Help, help!"

Unexpected onomatomes expressed the universal anguish. The child was implored by loud sobs. She was begged to say where she was and in what plight, whether dead, wounded, strangled, stabbed, cut in pieces, so much so and so wildly that she no longer dared speak or stir, and thought that phantoms by legions, at the least, were in pursuit of this grandam who had until then faithfully adhered to the sensible manners, the impeccable bearing, that made up the good old days of wasp waists and bustles. But the gallop came closer, and the little girl, whose anxiety became more acute with each strike of the heels, was already almost sure that death, but a death that bore no resemblance to Cynthia, a death with a skull of ice, eyes made up too black, was about to make his appearance.

The hurricane had already flung open the door, and it threw on the sofa a poor creature shriveled up with fear, the hat awry, which very quickly, nonetheless, pulled itself together. A simple toss of the head from right to left and the lid of the cranium found its customary place, and the child noticed that the grandmother had not changed very much, despite the volubility of her speech:

"The cook may be dead, but you are alive. So I can breathe again. We must telephone the doctor, the chief of police, inform your grandfather and mother so that they get here as soon as possible; but first of all I want to kiss you, since you're here safe and sound. I was so terribly frightened. Why didn't you answer me? A bit more and your silence would have made me die of worry. There's no end to the catastrophes that are raining down on our family, and although I'm not superstitious by nature, how can I help becoming so after such blows? My child, we have been robbed. You understand that. Robbed. A little more and we would have been murdered. The strangest part of the whole thing is that last night, like a presentiment, I had a dream . . . yes, a dream.

"A dream, should I be worried by a dream?" she continued, rather proud that she could still give the flavor of Racine to her discourse; for if she had nothing of the cruel queen about her, she could, however, in the present emergency, compare herself to Athalie, for—as was the case with the daughter of Jezebel—she had seen her sleep disturbed by terrible and portentous signs. Wild dogs had not fought over the bones of a paint-daubed old woman, but in her dream a beast had played a very sinister role.

. . . For there, in honor of a dream it dominated, an owl was perched on the pediment of a thuja and rosewood wardrobe, wearing a long funereal veil that trailed to the carpet. The bird of ill omen sobbed, moaned, gave vent to such laments, that the one whom he had come to trouble was on the verge of losing her temper until, through the tears of the whimpering fowl, she suddenly saw gleaming the gaze of her own sister, the late mother of Cynthia.

Moved, and at the same time exasperated, by this noisy display of despair, she made a charitable effort to be pleasant and asked her untimely caller not to stay any longer so uncomfortably perched. But hardly had she urged the owl to settle down for the night in a good armchair than, far from seeming touched by this gracious attention, the owl burst out laughing in her face and pointed to its feathered belly.

"You're being nice because you think I'm your sister, but I'm an owl. So then if I'm your sister, who are you?"

As it was not the hour for personal reflections, it was decided to let the owl talk, without giving ear to its discourse, but suddenly here was our fowl raising its voice and whistling threats. She was then called on to state clearly what she was driving at. Of course, it was enough to ask her for an explanation for her suddenly to shut up, and although there were neither windows nor doors open, she flew away, vanished, only the devil knows how, through the wall. But long after her departure, the widow's veil remained, floating in an oriflamme of woe.

On awakening, the old lady had restored her spirits with three teaspoonfuls of Melissa water from the monastery of the barefooted Carmelites, and then, as the clock indicated five, a little sleeping pill.

But the agony of dawn repeated the dream.

The uneventful morning offered a short respite: care of the rosebushes, the usual brief time on the belvedere. After lunch, throat contracted, hands restless, legs tingling with impatience, and a thousand other forewarnings of catastrophe. Then a visit to her friends at the Villa des Soupirs was decided on. One knows what followed. Once home, no one answered. Driven by some irresistible force, the grandmother went to the little blue *salon*. Why to the little blue *salon* rather than to the billiard room, the dining room, or the library? There, from the threshold, disorder, and she understood at once what it was the owl of her dream had wished to convey by its threats: the house had been burglarized.

"Do you hear, darling, burglarized? The little cabinet of souvenirs has been broken open. All that is left is one of your mother's first teeth. It was doubtless not out of delicacy that the bandits left it, for they took a bracelet made of the Empress Eugénie's hair. But how is it nothing is disturbed here? Didn't they come in?"

"No."

"Then you didn't see them?"

"No."

"Did you at least hear them?"

"No."

"Did the dog bark?"

"No."

"Strange. Bizarre. We must tell all this to the police. But let us recapitulate. They have stolen a bracelet made of the Empress Eugénie's hair. The cook is lying on the pantry floor, tied up like a leg of mutton. From the door I could see blood practically everywhere. You can well imagine, I didn't dare go any further. All I can hope is that the blood is not the girl's but the blood of the chicken we were supposed to have for dinner. If the poor girl were dead, the dog would be howling. No doubt it would have been better to have cut the ropes. But I, I would never have the courage. Let's lock ourselves in. That is wiser.

There now, stay near me while I telephone the police and your grandfather."

The grandmother at the telephone. The little girl suddenly felt frustrated. In an effort to revive the wind, she had passed the entire afternoon following the lovers in mid-ocean, while in a neighboring room someone had been stealing a bracelet braided from the Empress Eugénie's hair.

The Empress Eugénie . . .

Drifting in Cynthia's wake, among islands flowering with mold, on oceans too blue bordering on green, rose, and yellow continents, a noise, a shock of light emerging like an unexpected reef, had arrested her fine ship, "The Dream," and the child, forced to abandon Mr. and Mrs. Phosphorus to their miracle of sea, left the liquid kingdom only for the more imponderable one of ether. At least twenty times she had reread the story of the brother and sister without father or mother, who were obliged, because of the infamy of their guardian, to take flight in a balloon.

Orphans, balancing in the gondola of your balloon, don't laugh too hard at a surprise that reminds you of the astonishing flotilla of little boats that do not navigate on water but leap from earth to sky. Gone, alas, the joyous memory of fairs, of merry-go-rounds, of nougats, and vendors of sweets. A gimlet strong enough to pierce the hardest metal, thunder split the clouds and brought about the birth of serpents of fire; lightning, how could it not get the better of a silken sphere? The gale shook out a flaming head of hair, a head of hair it was not easy to tame, and not one curl of it would ever be twisted as inoffensive ornament around a wrist. The two urchins lost in the strands of this fleece of death weighed no more than two little fleas. To make themselves still lighter in the fury of the squall, they threw away their ballast, their clothes. Thus, amid hail and lightning, they shivered with cold at the same time that they roasted. Finally, the storyteller took pity. A cloudburst extinguished their delirium and the balloon dropped into a field so deeply ploughed that the fall was a gentle one. These shipwrecked survivors of the sky, in compensation for all their miseries, were to find on the banal soil of men the success of the avenged.

Thus the orphan girl, in the age of crinolines, made necklaces, belts, and pendants out of poppies, cornflowers, and other blossoms whose rural grace would permit her adolescence to shine forth at balls while sacrificing nothing of her modesty. So off we go to the Tuileries and its butterflies of gas. The Empress Eugénie, who had already noticed her, took her as one of her maids-of-honor. Uniforms, frivolities, a whole year passed like a farandole before the cold surprise of dawn. In a little while, one would be eating cats and rats. But what of it: forward two, for the quadrille!

Kilometers of tulle, hemispherically shaped from the pole of the waist to the equator, cut short by the surprise of the floor, had secrets of which the cavaliers knew nothing until dawn and its chilly temptation in the depths of landaus upholstered in white satin. A parquet made itself into a mirror so as to reflect the imperial splendors and gaieties, but all the same its varnished compliance did not reveal the mystery of the skirts that skimmed across it. The feet of the lovely waltzers were no more visible than the fire that crystallizes diamonds in the center of the earth. Chain of ladies, mauve, pink, and blue bouquet of waltzers, you whirl lightly on, awaiting the riot, that Cyclops who will undo you with a simple pressure of the thumb, without pity for the catastrophe of undone coiffures, uncurled ring-lets, heads of hair sweeping the ground, their poor roots in the grip of an authentic earthsickness.

The corolla of your skirts, their silky rustling perfumed with patchouli, wide open to the frenzied nostrils of the rabble, will intoxicate with a new drunkenness the swillers of red wine, and they will no more hear your screams, my beauties, than you heard the howls of the peonies whose murder stained the azure of your opalescence with too cloying, too heavy drops of blood. How could the terror of the black silken pistils of your legs, offered to their crude embraces, temper with pity the hands of the carriers of water? Once their relentless teeth are planted in the flesh that bloomed forth from a sheath of tender silk, it will be time enough to repent the low-cut bodices burst-ing with a triumph of breasts and the milky globes of shoul-ders, that will enflame the brutal passions of these men. Not until the last minute, to be sure, will anyone have foreseen these justified attacks, and, in homage to the whitest skins of Europe, diamonds, sapphires, rubies, and gems of every kind will have continued to blaze.

Multicolored fairyland, curves of fireworks repeated to in-finity in the pendants of the glass chandeliers, an Emperor and an Empress, wishing to take advantage of what still remained to them, opened the ball.

Despite the joyous fol-de-rols, they, of course, relinquished nothing of that superior, rather stiff demeanor, both the sign and the ransom of all earthly majesty. Brother and sister in magnificence to those elephants that, according to medieval bestiary fables, have no joints in their legs (thanks to which, for example, once the mastodon has been successfully brought to the ground by means of sawing down the tree against which

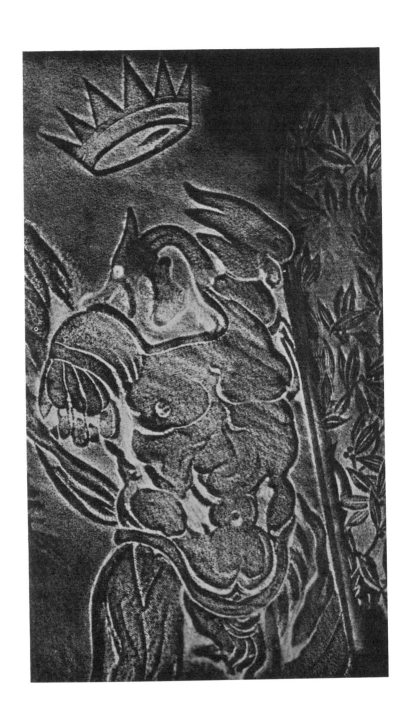

he sleeps standing, because deprived of the help of hamstrings, he becomes the easiest of prey for hunters), so these sovereigns were seemingly too inherently arrogant to let it be thought their legs were made of several sections hinged at the ankles and knees. Carved from a single piece, from even the most precious of human matter, marionettes that, by the bedizenment of decorations, medals of every kind, the crown diamonds, brocades and cameos, they revolved in a radiance compared to which mirrors exposed to the full light of the sun would have seemed dull.

And who could imagine anything more beautiful than the Empress? From hips to décolleté, a shadow of lace suggested the pinkest of secrets. As for the crinoline, as white as Chantilly lace is black, as ample and mysterious as it was complaisant and revealing, its reserve enhancing the haughty triumph of a bosom that the Emperor himself, despite the hierarchical character of the dance, could not keep from peering at. But in all justice it must be said that if he let his glance linger on the marvels that grazed his uniform, not for a second did he dream of taking the rhythm as excuse for pressing them closer. Besides, Their Majesties who open a ball must cut their wrists, or their lips, rather than yield to any one of those temptations so natural to the common herd that the little girl was not in the least surprised the first time she saw the gardener savagely biting the chambermaid's neck. But suppose the teeth of the Emperor had dared make such an audacious attack on the throat or the nape of the Empress's neck, the latter would not be the kind of woman to cluck contentedly as did the servant in her ravisher's embrace.

After the ball, when the Tuileries were again empty, doubtless the blonde Eugénie would permit her majestic spouse to play with a head of hair spread out for him alone. Like a river that the cup of his hands could not hold, the blondness would slip through his amorous fingers. Of that fleece on which the eyes of the world had been fixed there remained only a plait so narrow that by the time it came, by way of inheritance, into their possession, the grandmother and her sister had been unable to divide it, and Cynthia's mother had to content herself with a simple wisp of hair from the head of the small imperial prince.

Cynthia wore until this day the tiny frail pigtail on her forefinger, as others might wear a wedding ring; a wedding ring no lover could be jealous of since the Zulus had killed Eugénie's son. Zulus are giants the color of cart grease, with rings in their noses, and a small topknot on the summit of a shaved skull. With their arrows they assassinate explorers, then sit in a circle around a big fire and sing "Zulu, zulu, zulu," while the prisoners slowly cook. The Zulus are cannibals, but if the grandmother, who couldn't distinguish the blood of a chicken from that of a cook (whom she had, moreover, compared to a shoulder of mutton), had been served a thumb, being told it was the drumstick of some fowl, or been given a piece of the arm in the guise of filet of veal, would she not have eaten this flesh? A possible martyrdom already endowed the cook with the same dignity as that of a young man whose corpse browned on a fire as steady and monotonous as the song of the savages:

"Zulu, zulu, zulu, zulu ..." The servant was so fat, so flushed, that had the bandits disemboweled her, the blood would have flowed from her wound, as from an actual spigot, for at least a good quarter of an hour. "Zulu, zulu, zulu, zulu, gurgle-gur-gur." If she were dead, the most beautiful memories she would carry to the grave would be the edifying fairy scenes on the cover of the "Veillées des Chaumières." As for him, the little prince, merely to have breathed his mother's hair when she had kissed him before going to open the ball must have given him dreams for his whole lifetime. The burglars who stole the precious lock of hair, doubtless because of its gold clasp, did not know what marvel they had in their possession. Now they fled at top speed into the countryside as it turned mauve. The grandmother telephoned so that others would set off in pursuit. And what would become of them? In the bookcase moldered illustrated papers fifteen years old that told the story of a terrible gang of young men, young men who stole autos, then sneaked across the country at insane speeds, without pity for any who barred their way. The provincial calm of small towns was suddenly shaken by a great uproar, banks were ransacked, cobblestones bloodied, rifle shots turning to tragedy a hypocritical springtime in the Ile-de-France; reading the account of the prowess of the murderers it was impossible not to hope that these inexorable lads would not be caught. Fright invented epithets to blacken the names of conquistadors who had lost their way in a bureaucratic century. But Hannibal with his soldiers, his elephants, did he set out on any more just a conquest? Alas, pink-cheeked bandits, weariness soon bowed your proud shoulders, and then came betrayal. Some chose voluntary death, others endured to resign themselves to the terrible wait for the guillotine (and the sly curiosity of men and women who came to see judgment meted out); to wait before the blade fell on the neck, to wait interminable hours in cells under prison yards that smelled of wet paper.

And all these tortures for having wanted to revive the wind . . .

CHAPTER THREE

The Kerosene Drinker

Gathered around the cook, whom they had just unbound, the entire family listened to the story of the owl.

Because she already knew the marvelous secrets of dreams, the child soon accepted her grandmother's as a matter of course. But she was the only one who did, and the others, the grandfather, the mother, and the *gendarmes* could make nothing of it at all. So the storyteller, sensing the quasiunanimity of the audience at her mercy, made every possible effort (new kind of Orpheus that she was) to draw her docile listeners into forests of mystery and terror.

The dismay written on each face gave her some indication of the measure of her success, but she avoided the glance of a little girl who understood all too well the strange farce of memory, and who remembered that only yesterday this inspired creature was explaining her state of mind in scientific and incomprehensible terms borrowed from her learned husband. Now, however, perjuring the whole of a positivistic past, the new sibyl threw to the winds in a single gesture all those sharp deductions, those logical, sure-fire weapons that hit the mark, as well as the arrow of reason and all that made up the arsenal of her customary arguments. A brand-new scorn prevented her from using terms and references that had validated her entire life. Moreover, she lost nothing in this exchange, for she had forgotten her initial terror on the kitchen threshold at the sight of the garroted body, which the promise of an empire could not have persuaded her to touch. She was able to affirm, and in all sincerity, that on the battlefield of the tiles she had felt as much at her ease and as majestic as Napoleon at Austerlitz. The stains that blossomed in sinister conjecture the length of the walls, stains that had made her wonder if they were the blood of chicken or servant, she added to the bouquet of her presentiments.

She was aware in each of her senses of a power of penetration equal to that of the X-ray, and for a little while she saw herself as absolute mistress of the destinies that surrounded her. Consequence: the cook, who believed herself already in the tomb, suddenly felt herself reborn thanks to an energetic: "You're alive, my girl, you haven't been assassinated."

On the second or third repetition of this simple sentence, little by little, one by one, the cook recovered her wits. And now here she was walking with a vigorous step past the circle of the family and constabulary to return to her saucepans. This *Cordon Bleu* mysteriously resuscitated, the red-faced girl putting the bread to soak for the soup would undoubtedly have slipped into oblivion had not her mistress fished her out and obliged her to go on living.

Weep, weep with joy, weep with pride, weep in triumph, Whitsuntide serving-girl; was the blue flame of the gas range about to come and fold itself around a brow that, for sixty long years, had allowed none but severely restricted thoughts to enter, hypotheses without brilliance, deductions so prudent as to appear dull? But such humility, for those who have eyes to perceive it, is at all times the announcer of a great destiny. The burglary had been like Newton's apple, a dolorous apple, no doubt, but since the scene of the crime incites alimentary comparisons, does not the wisdom of nations say that an omelette was never made without the breaking of eggs? Moreover, had the apple fallen on Newton's nose instead of stupidly to the ground, who knows if the modality of this fall would not have given us two discoveries instead of one? Whether neither or nor, the reign of monotony was done with. A colorless era had come to a close. And now on to elegance, to strange whims and their surprises and miracles! A servant was the first to benefit from this outpouring, and she was already preparing a lyrical repast. It was enough to see her peeling her potatoes to grasp that she was now porous to the most subtle emanations. The family and the constabulary had learned on whom, from then on, their fate depended.

Breathing was oppressed, hearts pounded like beating drums, for there was something prodigious in the air. Talk of Cleopatra's nose, of Pascal, as much as you liked, but the faithful and hitherto realistic spouse of the Third Republic's most celebrated psychiatrist knew that the strumpets, the Cynthias, were not the only ones to benefit, for their own personal use, from certain gifts. Outside, the mass of a summer night weighed on the gardens, but the burden of it did not crush, or even so much as crumple, the mysteries of the house (vulnerable though they were), for already, silent and invisible, an entire gulf stream was spreading its magnetic waves. From the chaos of a kitchen ransacked by bandits came spinning an unexpected hope. The *gendarmes* of the Ile-de-France, strapped in their uniforms, opened their mouths wide, the better to hear! A materialistic and dogmatic seventy-year-old man, listening to his lifetime mate, suddenly felt his most imperious convictions crumbling. A young woman who had not as yet suffered in her body from being deprived of love, found no better way to still the sudden and nervous hunger of her fingers than to stroke the hair of a little girl who listened without flinching to the invocation to the stars, the planets. Their too dazzling joy would presently cause them one and all to tremble, as if the sky, summoned as witness, was no more than an enormous injustice in the teeth of the moon.

Bird of sinister augury, veiled like a widow, from the pinnacle of a thuja and rosewood wardrobe as if on some ill-omened Olympus, what spell did your eyes, gleaming with a familiar look, cast on this family? The police officer himself, belted, booted, was so affected that he asked that, before starting the investigation, a few drops of cologne be sprinkled on his handkerchief to restore his spirits. And now, to put himself at ease, he twirled his mustaches, but he was still far from being in control. He kept an eye on the stove, as if expecting legions of owls to fly out of it. Only the child maintained her poise. From the bottom of her heart, she was thankful to the aunt with the feathered belly and the long veil, for it was due to her that the monotony of the days had at last been broken. Behind the head of this new mystic a copper warming pan formed a tawny halo and, moved by so much majesty, the old and learned man sought in the confusion of his mind some prop for his tottering faith that would fortify his already weakened submission to facts and at the same time not rob her who bore his name of her unsuspected grandeur. In all conscience and with logic, he sought the reasons that might have induced his deceased sister-in-law to thus metamorphose herself into an owl.

"Perhaps this is a new trick of Cynthia's. Still, we always did our duty by her."

"If anyone has anything to reproach himself with, it's certainly not us."

"Well, then?"

"Well, then," resumed the grandmother, "this combination of events troubles me all the more because, if we always were, my dear sister and I, like two fingers of the same hand, still I must confess that on one occasion, on the death of our cousin from Compiègne (whose two sole heirs we were), we had a scene, and a very violent one, and precisely because of the bracelet of the Empress Eugénie's hair, which each of us wanted to keep. I invoked my right of primogeniture, whereupon she replied that my republican convictions hardly qualified me to be a fit depository for an imperial relic. Unable to come to an agreement, we drew lots for the bracelet. Luck was with me, and never again did my poor sister or I speak of the discussion we had had on the subject. So, coming in a little while ago, I knew from the minute I was in the front hall what had happened, and do you know which room I went to first? I rushed to the blue salon and straight to the glass case that contained the memento. It was no longer there. Its place was empty. The bandits had taken the bracelet . . ."

The family choir resumed the funereal strain:

"The bracelet . . ."

"Yes, the bracelet, the bracelet of the Empress Eugénie's hair."

"A bracelet of the Empress's hair."

"Of the Empress's hair, you have said it, my girl."

"Madame can believe that I would rather they killed me, if only I could have prevented them from taking it. When I saw them, I said to them: 'You'll have to pass over my dead body before you'll get away with something that doesn't belong to you.' Then those scamps laughed to split their sides, and as for her, Madame, she called me an old bag."

"*She*, what she? So there was a woman in the band?"

"To be sure, Madame, and I even cursed her out. I'm only a poor wretch of a cook, but it didn't keep me from cursing her out before heaven and earth. After all that Monsieur and Madame did for her!"

"So we know her then?"

"Does Madame know her! What surprises me is that Madame with her second sight hasn't already guessed."

"Keep quiet! I know, I know: Lucie, the little chambermaid . . ."

"Once more Madame has hit the nail on the head. Yes, Madame, the chambermaid and her boyfriend, the assistant gardener, and a bunch of their cronies besides. Many's the day my heart was heavy as lead. If I'd known, I'd have spoken out long ago, but I was stupid out of goodness. At first, I suspected nothing. What with her lowered eyes and her innocent air, but watch out for saintly hypocrites . . . First of all, the moods she had, that girl. Some days she'd be a real bitch, and other times it would be lovey this and lovey that, so I never knew which leg

I was standing on. And then she liked to loaf too much. I tried
to find excuses for her: she's anemic, I used to tell myself. It's a
fact she did have a papier-mâché look. Well, a lot of good it
does to plaster your mug with rouge when you've been jigging
around until three in the morning ... In Paris every night it
was a ball here and a ball there, and I dance you this way and
dance you that. More often than not, she didn't come back
before daybreak, and Sunday afternoon, so as to get some rest,
it was the movies. She put on such airs when we came here
you'd have thought she was off her nut. But was I her mother
to keep her from pouring whole spoonfuls of vinegar into
everything she ate? It's like with the mustard. She spread layers
of it on her bread, bit square into the middle of the slice, enough
to make all the devils in hell sneeze, and then blubbered like a
magdalene. Life's sad enough already without forcing yourself
to eat things that bring tears to your eyes. But try to make that
pigheaded creature listen to reason. One day I came into my
kitchen and she was sucking a piece of coal, and another time,
I couldn't believe my eyes, she was drinking kerosene. The
night of the kerosene she was sick, sick as a dog. Then I per-
mitted myself to make a passing remark. She answered me
back that she was doing like Madame's niece, Mademoiselle
Cynthia, who drank and smoked and sniffed all kinds of filth,
and Lucie told me the names, such queer names I can't remember them. All the time the redhead was here, Lucie would
pinch her stuff, take a good smacking dose, then close her eyes
and think she was in paradise. But I, I told her all those schemes
were no more or less than poison, and if she was so stuck on
imitating someone she'd do better not to pick out Cynthia.
Ouitche. She was crazy about her, and when she couldn't rummage anymore through her bazaar of vices—and because, sav-

ing your presence, she was set on going nuts—she ate coal and guzzled tumblerfuls of kerosene. Madame can well believe that I asked myself more than once where such tastes could have come from. I was always asking her about her family. She didn't like that subject. All she ever told me was that she had a brother who must have had something to do with aviation because he was, after what she told me, a '*monte-en-l'air*.' "*

Lucie, the kerosene drinker, was quite as pretty in her white apron as the little maids in American films. The child could still see her sitting in the linen room with a song on her lips. "*Les-monte-en-l'air*."† That fat fool of a cook understood nothing about anything, and the little chambermaid's smile had been so wan, so gentle when, for a little girl who knew her secret and how to keep it, she sang a song with words sadder than the winter rain on the roof, the song of the *monte-en-l'air*. Tears had shone in those eyes that bread spread with mustard had long since accustomed to the voluptuous torture of weeping.

Frail little drinker of kerosene, a child listened to the tale of your *monte-en-l'air*, that sturdy and supple lad who was as brave as they come. Surprised while visiting an apartment, he got out through a window and wandered for hours over the roofs of Paris. His white espadrilles with their blue ribbons stood out in the night, meowing cats scampered between his legs, and twenty times, thanks to them, he almost broke his neck. The cold nipped his muscles to the bone, but the police had had to wait until dawn and its bitter treacheries to get the better of his courage. At last they caught him. For months and

*Translator's note: *Monte-en-l'air* is archaic slang, meaning "burglar" or "second-story worker."

†Translator's note: Crevel uses the plural article in the title of the song, doubtless because "monte" is not a noun.

months he was closed away in prison, where, little by little, all those who wanted to revive the wind die from silence and immobility.

In order to forget her sorrows, his oversensitive sister had rummaged through Cynthia's cupboards. What she found there restored her self-confidence, and also the gardener liked to kiss her on the neck. Alas, it was their misfortune not to have a groat between them, and lovers can't live within four bare walls. So, like the father and Cynthia, they decided to go away. So as not to die of hunger en route, they took forks and spoons with them, a silver service nobody ever used, and, because they had good taste and were sentimental, they added to this hardware the bracelet made of Empress Eugénie's hair. But so the fugitive would not be cold in the car that made hope rise in tremors so light, so light on the roads of impenetrable night, the gardener ("he has the strength of two," the grandmother had said of him that very morning as she saw him digging in the garden) would hold her very tight to keep her warm. And if she closed her eyes, she would see millions of stars.

Love, love, flight at breakneck speed, the father and Cynthia left like robbers, the robbers left like the father and Cynthia. Two couples must have cried aloud for joy when, at the first curve of the road, the ennui of that building and the arrogance of the poplars became invisible forever. Two couples, that is eight slightly mad eyes. Men accept to feel themselves enslaved by those slender creatures, their companions. Cleopatra, they say, liked to wind snakes around her wrists. That's better than bracelets made of the hair of the Empress. If the game turned out badly for that African lady, it was because she wanted it to. Cynthia and the little chambermaid had less theatrical tastes, and neither had they any need of battles on the high seas to know about miraculous tempests.

Let the wind subside; they could revive themselves with drugs from their strange boxes, from their secret flacons. Imagine, the fat, stupid cook couldn't even remember what should be breathed, drunk, smoked, in order to discern the sun whose flames gilded these lovers! Wavering hopes, dreams still uncertain as to what to cling to, words had to be invented that would be worthy of baptizing the ecstasies, the lyrical thunderbolts, that the child wanted, later, to traverse her life. She would doubtless never have the courage to drink kerosene, but she knew very well that her boredom, so as to get tipsy, would find again those philters that made Cynthia's eyes so profoundly unfathomable. Happiness, apotheosis. Then she would be avenged for the days, the weeks, the months, the years, of waiting. Echoes from every corner of the world would prolong the thunder of unforgettable minutes. Nevermore those dinners at a joyless table. Already this evening, the simple flight of a chambermaid in love had lit unhoped-for planets in the habitual monotony. How difficult patience is! In a little while, after the grandmother's harangue, and the questioning of the cook, and the customary verifications, after the police were gone, the child felt almost envious of these burly, mustachioed men for whom the night opened wide. And now a disdainful glance at a slice of cold veal, and she regretted more than ever that, with hygiene as a pretext, mustard had been banished from this house. Small revenge that the grandfather, happy to have found new reasons for disparaging Cynthia, did not even wait for the vegetables to provide the names the cook had stupidly forgotten.

"A fine state of affairs!" stormed the man of science. "And

when I think that these scandalous scenes were staged in my house! I learn that Cynthia was not content with being a dissolute, shameless woman. She was in addition a drug addict. No doubt she was cleverly perverse enough to win over you know whom by her charming habits. We who drink only water could scarcely compete with a creature who offered the ominous luxury of her artificial paradises. What the devil could she have taken? Cocaine, opium, morphine, ether? See the example: Lucie, at first an irreproachable servant, started drinking kerosene! She became a kerosene addict. By the way, I shall call attention to this curious perversion at some meeting of the Academy of Medicine. Unfortunately, I won't be able to cite other instances, and my information will not be well substantiated. Deductions should be made with the utmost caution. Let's see for a moment. I have treated all kinds of drug addicts. A common characteristic: some here, some there can be recognized by their amorality, which in no way prevents certain specific deviations. As for kerosene addicts, I believe them to be voluntary thieves, as cocaine addicts are liars, morphine maniacs badly groomed, opium fiends sedentary . . ."

"Kerosene addicts, thieves. That's a fine discovery! At least no one could accuse you of having compromised yourself by the audacity of your hypothesis," hissed the grandmother. "The cook herself would make the same diagnosis. A kerosene drinker makes off with priceless family heirlooms, and the conclusion you come to is: kerosene addicts are thieves! Bravo. I admire your powers of deduction. They make one marvel! The only trouble is we don't know which way to turn. Enough of this nonsense and be honest enough to admit that you, a celebrated psychiatrist, and a mechanic of the soul, can throw no more light on this happening than the first cop to come along.

For more than thirty years I had a blind faith in you. I believed you were a great psychiatrist. Well, this occurrence will have at least served the sad purpose of having opened my eyes. I now perceive my naiveté, my stupidity. Your knowledge is an empty word, good for nothing at all."

"What, what, my good woman? Is it possible?"

"It is possible, and I have said what I mean. Open your eyes. You've brought yourself and us to a pretty pass. Let us recapitulate. You choose for your daughter a boy without principles. Cynthia comes to live with us. You find her charming, perfect, until the day she kidnaps our son-in-law. That day, strong and determined, you come to the inevitable conclusion. Inevitable, what is the inevitable? Permit me to laugh. You pretend to be subservient to facts, but you could live to be a hundred and never learn anything about them. Your home goes from bad to worse, and had I by chance been murdered today you would have been unable to give a list of the stolen objects. But, thanks be to heaven, I am here, very much alive, with my arms and legs still flesh and bone. Presently order will be put into this state of affairs."

"But, my good woman, what is all this about? I don't understand."

"If you don't understand, I ask nothing better than to explain things to you. From now on, I alone will be in control of this house. I shall be the mistress and completely the mistress. Since my dream, and since my presentiments were proven true, I am another woman. I am aware of my value and I will no longer be subjected to your methods. Listen to me. Your experimental procedures, your precious deductions, I don't give a snap of the fingers for them. I believe in genius, in intuition. You are no longer my idol."

"That I am no longer your idol, my good woman, I well understand. Thank God the practice of science has made me very humble. Painful though it may be to me, I do not complain of your attitude, at least as far as I myself am personally concerned. But you, you, dear friend, the companion of my labors for a third of a century, don't you feel there is something a little flighty just the same in this sudden and complete change? You may recall my theory about mushroom-acts. You know that I reserve this term for everything that manifests an activity, if not contrary to, at least quite different from the one we are logically entitled to expect. I will make myself clear: mushroom-acts are all the acts that have no more rational causes than the mushroom has roots. Both stand a good chance of being poisonous, even though imprudent people relish them. Moreover, it is simple justice that the most spontaneous of plants should be the one least firmly attached to the soil that nourishes all vegetation. Thus, mushroom-acts, which the scatterbrained are fond of lauding for their rapid growth and dazzling appearance (and which they often connect with I know not what more or less extravagant notion of liberty), these mushroom-acts, I tell you, because nothing wise, nothing certain fixes them either in time or space, despite the impression their sudden appearance makes on the shifting mind of man, we know how long their action can last. The fact that Alcibiades had his dog's tail cut off, an eccentricity that caused a three-day uproar in the city, demonstrates but one thing in the eyes of future generations—the sole judges that I recognize—and that is the unstable disposition of the perpetrator . . ."

Poor old scholar, lost in his theory of mushroom-acts, fought step by step for a domestic authority they were trying to cheat him of. Never had he held on to it so strongly until the minute he felt it threatened. Regret wrinkled, zebra-striped his face. A like tremor had in olden days disfigured the face of Greece the day the wind of fire parched the Ilissus, burned the peaceful illusion of the olive trees, blasted the wisdom of the Philosophers, and trusted in the echoes of a world that was to invent socks, advertising billboards in the countryside, autobuses, crises of conscience, venereal diseases, tinned lobster *à l'octopus*, mutton stew, rubber heels, and the nutcracker:

Pan, the great Pan is dead.

Because of this lament, in the jumble of ancient gods, of Spartan heroes and Athenian generals, a little girl remembered only Pan. Eurythmic robes were torn, the carefree strength of athletes defiled, as well as the whitest of white wools, things having gone so far as to deprive the dead of their cakes of honey. In meager compensation, from then on they were granted the honor of black veils, those long veils that reach down to the ground when, from the top of a wardrobe with a looking-glass door, the mother of the last of the pagans came to forecast woe.

Pan, the great Pan is dead.

Pan, who dared defy Phoebus. Slowly the Eleusinian stars were extinguished. The flawless profiles became distorted. Misfortune and owls watched over the universe. Dead were the pythonesses with hair of vipers, those beautiful inspired creatures with fiery mouths and fluid gaze. Today a domesticated witch invokes the secret powers solely to threaten the lovers and send the police of the Seine-et-Oise in their pursuit. However successful the ball of the Tuileries may have been, was an imperial luminary's curl worth depriving of their only possible happiness two young people who didn't have thirty-six ways of living close to each other without the torment of daily servitude?

After the copious report on the theory of mushroom-acts, the grandmother, who had definitely forsworn grave and modest ideals, once again affirmed her newborn faith in genius and intuition. She talked of a young magistrate she had caught a glimpse of that afternoon at her friends of the Villa des Soupirs, and how was it possible not to thank heaven for this discovery named Petitdemange? It was Petitdemange this, Petitdemange that. She was sure he would find the burglars, give advice, addresses, a philosophy, and, in short, provide all that is requisite to the material and spiritual life of a family. Petitdemange was at the same time the name of a clown, of a catastrophe, or of a cannibal, thought the child, who was to dream all night of this unknown person who was about to join the coalition against a sentimental gardener and his pretty drinker of kerosene. Petitdemange's laugh, which she could not as yet connect with any face, stabbed her sleep with a thousand menaces. But how to protect those whose passion tears them from the aid of walls and laws? The tenderness of the sleeping child was a fragile paper screen whose transparent defense Petitdemange rips with a flick of a finger. Highways belong to the lovers of the entire world. The wind nourishes their lungs, lights up their glances. But what hole in the horizon will permit them to escape and scale the stars?

Like a curtain, there rises up into the heavens the flowers that had been so carelessly strewn. Far up on high, purple calyxes sway, and among the clouds a Montgolfier balloon dances in its crinoline. An auto turning redder and redder is a dizzy stain of madness on the ribbons and nets of tar that keep the countryside from flying away. By morning the wind, which the loftiest of creatures believe is their life-breath, had scattered their forces. And they fall to earth, on the hard earth, on the cold earth, marionettes from a lugubrious circus. They are laid in a long box mounted on two wheels, and a small ivory horse draws them in jolts across a desolate land. Soon they are at the threshold of a forest of stones. There the soil loses forever that vegetal sweetness that plants relinquish in exchange for the invisible nourishment they receive. Pebbles, flint, scrap iron, but the hoof of an ivory horse does not fear the avenues of cruelty, nor does his brow fear the flames of that sun that is about to crash into letters of the most inexorable apple-green, on a pink that sets one's teeth on edge, the pink of the box in which lie the marionettes. *Puppets in Love* announce the planks of this coffin of joint tenancy.

Puppets in love, and, the better to jeer at them, all the wickednesses of the entire world seat themselves in a circle at the most desolate crossroad, shaking with a laughter akin to the laughter of Petitdemange. Whoa, there, ivory horse! It's time to open the box. You see, it's mere child's play. The hinged lid slides back of its own accord.

Flesh rumpled, eyes blinking, all the famous couples rise up for their paltry resurrections. An unhoped-for revenge: the only ones to have retained a possible hope are Cynthia, fresher than a lemon ice despite her long, torn, golden train, and the father, so debonair, with the tails of his dress jacket more bedraggled than the wings of a drenched bird; and a little chambermaid, the drinker of kerosene, and her lover, the gardener.

CHAPTER FOUR

Another Idyll

On the following morning, there being no chambermaid to carry breakfast to their rooms, the family gathered very early around the dining-room table. A good pretext to hold a conventicle. This assembly in pajamas and dressing gowns reminded the child of those after the battle bivouacs as described and pictured in books consecrated to the wars of the First Empire.

Although this was the day after a severe ordeal, no one looked as if he had met his Waterloo. The grandfather himself feigned to have forgotten the upbraiding of the night before, and the newborn sybil, without relinquishing any of her classical authority, included in her morning greetings the happy prophecies of a dream. In fact, that night the sleep of many had its visitors. So now it was the cook's turn to make the acquaintance of the owl. But in her attic room the bird of ill omen had found no wardrobe upon which to perch, and, lacking a pulpit worthy of the one whose spirit she incarnated, had quickly taken flight again, and in the worst of humors. From there, the defunct and winging soul, unable to roost on the heights, went down to the grandmother's floor without, however, neglecting to change her dress. Rid of her crêpe, more elusive than a reflection on the water, she dazzled the eyes of the sleeper when she made her appearance in the shape of a magic fish, perfectly at ease on the mirror that served as pond.

Little lake, held smoothly between the banks of thuja and rosewood, the mirror suddenly lost its boundaries, and because the time of sinister portents was past, the heroine of this aquatic dream quite simply and frankly introduced herself: "I am a goofy gudgeon." A belly of white scales illuminated the serene and marvelous waters of the dream. Nothing was easier than to question the fraternal spirit detected within this guise.

"What quirk of destiny has compelled you today to take this shape to visit me?"

"I escaped from a river."

"From which river?"

"The river of happiness."

"The river of happiness? I want to bathe in its waters. What is its name? What country does it flow through?"

"The river of happiness has no name. It flows through no country."

"How then can I ever come to know it?"

"As long as you insist, oh, my sister, for you I shall forego the mute customs of fish. The river that I, a fish of portent, escaped from tonight, this river comes from no unfeeling glacier or from no ordinary spring, but from a proud and noble face. For

you and your home, so long afflicted, happiness flows in torrents from a royal beard. From this it should be easy to perceive
from whence your salvation will come."

"His name, his name? I dare not say it."

"And you know it. You know that I refer to that young magistrate with a future whom you glimpsed this afternoon at the
Villa des Soupirs. You, yourself, haven't you already spoken of
him to your family?"

"Petitdemange."

"Petitdemange himself. Alfred Petitdemange."

"Thank you, oh, my sister, but don't leave again! Stay near
me, and, if you leave, let me hope that I shall see you soon
again."

"Nevermore, alas, shall I be able to return. Behold my scales,
behold my fins. You will remember that despite the rigid principles by which we were brought up by a thrifty and strait-
laced mother—you will remember that I (contrary to you) always had a taste for pretty dresses and big hats. However, it
wasn't just coquettishness that prompted me to don this aquatic
tea gown. Behold my spangles, behold my veils of tulle. The
parts of my body that do not glitter are completely transparent.
But in all this I find no reason to rejoice. I glide and glitter, but
this reincarnation will be the last, for it condemns me to everlasting nothingness. At dawn, all that is left to me of life shall
be torn from me, devoured, do you hear, eaten, masticated,
swallowed, and that by my own daughter, Cynthia. Cynthia,
shameless and naked in her lover's bed, her milk-white belly
girdled by the brown arm of he who was your son-in-law, her
legs entwined with those of the male against whom she so
furiously rubbed herself before she fell asleep; Cynthia, my
daughter, whose loves have not been blessed by marriage, is

remorseful while she sleeps, and at this very moment is admitting to herself that she is no better than a crane. A crane. Cranes, she believes, live on fish. Here you can see the danger of the metaphor of words. Thus was our great-aunt Laura made a demimondaine through the fault of a predestined name in a time when women who misbehaved were called 'lorettes.' As for the present epoch, because she leads a life that neither poverty nor bad example could have made her choose, my daughter is a crane.* What will become of me? Cynthia, my child, you are pardoned, but what a distressing spectacle! A life begun in scandal continues in crime. Oh, heavens, I am dying. She is eating me. Sh-she is-s-s eat-eat-eating m-me. Sh-sh-sh-sh-she i-i-i-i-s ea-t-t-i-n-g-g-g-g m-m-m-m-me."

Syllables, letters turn fluid. For one last time the echo repeats the hollow onomatopoeia, which, before her valorous death, had ebbed and flowed in the voice of an apparition that would never again appear. Waves of malediction, spume of dismay, everything from the depths was abolished on the surface of sleep. Scarcely a ripple on the ocean, and upon its silence there remained only a concentric dance of circles growing wider and wider, less and less distinct as after a drowning, a shipwreck.

Still it was fortunate that this final visitation confirmed the grandmother's first impression of Petitdemange. No more hesitating. It would be to him, to him alone and to no other, that the appeal must be made. What about telephoning him at once? It was still a bit early, however, to disturb this young, but solemn, magistrate. It was half-past eight by the clock. Half an hour from now would be perfect. Meanwhile, a bite of toast. An arrogant tooth attacked it. The tooth of a lion, it seemed,

*Translator's note: *Grue*, translated as "crane," has also the meaning, colloquially, "whore."

but a lion who would, in his glory, ferociously set no limits on himself. The samovar purred, its gentleness, its song, transformed into words, so light, so light; and because the entire family had abjured confidence, one single voice no longer waited to take wing and ask for the telephone number of the judge with a golden beard. He would drop by that afternoon. The phantom sister was right. A pity that she could not return. Her presentiments were of such help. But why was it that Cynthia, even in dreams, continued to heap crime upon crime? If only she didn't take it into her head to seize upon Petitdemange, the unhoped-for godsend. But could one ever know what to expect of the redheaded creature who had already carried off a son-in-law, or of the crane who had devoured the most clairvoyant of all fish-owls ever to haunt an earthly dream?

★
★ ★

The reign of Petitdemange.

Because the old lady felt nervous, the grandfather returned alone to his scientific work. She whom he had so proudly called his most devoted pupil and most intelligent collaborator spent the autumn with her mother on the estate in the Seine-et-Oise (the scene of the burglary, as it was now called, not without pride). Daily, or twice a day rather than once, Petitdemange visited these ladies. He became the court favorite, their ideal of the eternal masculine. They doted on him a little more with every passing hour. They even went so far as to see him as the spitting image of François Premier.

The child, not sharing in their enthusiasm, considered this newcomer overestimated, and pored over the illustrations, descriptions, and documents in her history books, and in the

Petit Larousse, to convince herself that there was no resemblance whatsoever between the conqueror of Marignan and the bearded neighbor who had become part of the coalition against Cynthia and the father, against the drinker of kerosene and her lover.

But how to prove to these infatuated women that their magistrate did not deserve so flattering a comparison? There was nothing to be done; Petitdemange confessed he was afraid of assassins, never went out without his revolver, closely scrutinized taxi drivers before entrusting them with his precious fate, never got into a bed without looking beneath it, and yet in one voice these women cried out: "How prudent! How wise! How right he is!"

If he spoke of a dirty trick done to a colleague, thanks to which his own promotion would be aided, they would remark, in perfect agreement: "Petitdemange is cleverer than Ulysses." If he were coming to lunch, the grandmother would begin as early as eleven o'clock to erect in his honor pyramids of peaches, pears, apples, grapes, and in so doing regret that autumn did not have a finer choice of fruit.

As she had somewhat forgotten her Gothic mythology, once the bowls of fruit were arranged, she asked:

"What is the name of the goddess of the harvest?"

"Ceres."

"Ceres, quite so."

And off she went to her daughter's door to tell her that with her own hands she had picked the best fruit in the orchard. "Our guest will believe he is in the realm of Ceres. The goddess of the harvest will be you. Wear your yellow organdy dress and under it a pink slip. You'll tell me that we're in the middle of autumn and that organdy . . . My darling, there are days in one's lifetime when one must take risks. We are enjoying a truly August sun. May its splendor be our ally. The pink of your slip underneath the yellow of the organdy will make such an impression on him that I would not be surprised, oh, not at all surprised, if Petitdemange did not propose today. Dear Alfred, an artist, as we well know, could not remain unmoved by the charm of such a warm pretty color, alluring without being provocative. You were wearing your bathing suit when you made the acquaintance of your first husband. At twenty you had slender hips. Today—not that I mean to say you are an old woman—but you are over thirty, and you have developed from a thin and nervous child into a calm and handsome young woman. Before long you will be quite imposing. Now a magistrate with a big future before him could not permit himself to be attracted to a bag of skin and bones. I could swear to it that Petitdemange, our dear Alfred, will choose a majestic mate. I can already picture you in a low-cut gown, wearing all our diamonds, all our lace, a respected, and even a wee bit envied, wife. Then, my darling, then we shall have our revenge on Cynthia! But there is not a moment to lose. So, in short: put on your yellow organdy dress, a pink slip underneath, and you will be as golden as Grecian marble, as the noonday sun, as Petitdemange's beard . . ."

And she told off an entire rosary of comparisons, all of the purest lyricism, while the young woman meekly got dressed. Once this was done, they went down to the *salon*. What a pity that the mahogany furniture refused to lend itself to the romanticism of a certain lively disorder. If you turned and twisted it about this way and that for hours you would barely succeed in making the house look as if it had not been put in order for at least six months. "The next time," announced the grand-

mother, "we'll invite him to dinner. I'll have Aunt Sophie's harp brought down from the attic. You will drape yourself in your long green scarf. A few scattered rose petals, a crystal vase, an open score upon the piano, a straw hat from Italy, as if by accident, on the sofa! All this will give us a touch of Malmaison. You remember at the Grévin Museum, a reception of Josephine's in the heyday of Rueil . . ."

The heyday of Rueil. The Creole Josephine, faithful to the diaphanous veils that make each woman a small cloud of light in the transparent evenings of Martinique. The child had not forgotten the Thursday when she had been taken to see the life-size wax dolls. The brown-haired Empress in her floating Grecian gown was a fitting rival for the other, the one with blond curls and crinoline. The *salon* opened upon a motionless blue night. Glances shadowed by mauve eyelids, hair in turbans, diadems, the suggestion of slim legs in the secrecy of long pleats, arms following the gentle curves of the furniture, these creatures had for all eternity their smiles, their ambitions, their happinesses. What could men and women know of them today? They could not hear the echoes in all this silence, although from a harpsichord that insensitive visitors had considered mute, fingers with nails rosier and more shapely than those on the attractive hands in the show-windows of beauty shops drew forth a melody whose freshness recalled a certain flower . . . Rose-geranium, which had given its name to Cynthia's perfume. Rose-geranium, a scent so subtle and so penetrating that at the time the red-haired cousin lived in the house three drops of it were sufficient to intoxicate Lucie, the drinker of kerosene.

The child knew that even were Aunt Sophie's harp brought down, and the score opened at this or that page, not even the contents of the elaborate bottles on the grandmother's dressing table were worthy of comparison with the unrivaled rose-geranium in its simple little bottle; thus in pursuit of Petitdemange, who was the prey they stalked, no gesture, no effort, could ever endow these two women with the mystery, the grace, that promised extraordinary resurrections—the faces, the bodies disdainfully impassive in their exile at the Grévin Museum more living in their wax than the actual flesh, the actual skin, of these breathing women.

The grandmother very quickly announced that too much pride might prove unlucky for them. "So sit down quite simply in that easy chair. Puff out your organdy. There could be nothing prettier than that yellow flounce that hints at a design of *toile de Jouy de Parme*. Take this rose between the thumb and forefinger of your left hand. A book in your right hand, but quickly, we must hurry. I hear an auto stopping outside. That must be he. If we had had the time we could have looked around for the volume of Musset. But here, here's a Baedeker. It's quite poetic, just the same. Trips to Italy, Venice, the Mediterranean, Sicily, yes, that will do, that will do. Look at the flower, smell the book. Heavens, I am so excited that words trip me up. Smell the flower, look at the book. I'm more wrought-up than if my own fate were at stake. You're the lucky one. Smile, smile. Good day, dear friend. Good day, how are you?"

Petitdemange kissed their hands.

The child felt pity for her mother, who sat congealed in all that yellow organdy, like a paper lantern they had forgotten to light on the Fourteenth of July.

★
★ ★

The entire family returned to Paris.

A bouquet of flowers arrived. It was put in the *salon*.

"At last we've got hold of a son-in-law, and, in my opinion, a good one this time," declared the cook. She announced the glad tidings to the servants in the apartment house, and described the husband-to-be: "He has a beard like the sun, he is all smiles, and his teeth shine so brightly in all that golden hair that it puts you in mind of a box of sardines in a wheat field at noon, in summer. It was the old girl who concocted the whole affair. There's one who's no dummy. She knows how to take care of herself, you bet. Not stuck up, but clever and crafty. A real Catherine de Médicis . . ."

The real Catherine de Médicis then sent for the little girl:

"Darling, I have something to say to you."

"Yes, I know it already. Mama is going to marry the man with the beard. Is she going to wear a veil and a white dress with a train? The new chambermaid says she hasn't the right . . ."

A harsh word silenced her questioner. But how to keep her from judging under her breath: "Petitdemange and Mama are engaged, but are not lovers . . . ," or from still and always thinking of her father, of Cynthia, Mr. Knife and Miss Fork, Mr. and Mrs. Phosphorus, who danced lightly, lightly at night over the crest of dreams . . .

The truth of it was that she who had maneuvered the whole affair, according to a servant's interpretation, did not appear any too pleased with her handiwork. However rapturously she might exclaim: "Aren't they delightful!" no conviction was in it. Furthermore, she was on the brink of a nervous collapse. Up until now, not a minute of her existence but had its purpose, its joy, its anger. But here she was getting a foretaste of ennui. Time was passing imperceptibly and monotonously. She had to admit to herself her uncertain state of mind. And the old positivistic husband was now so submissive that she no longer had the heart to carry on the discussion begun the night of the robbery. She compared herself to the creator. But to a creator who did not require six days to complete his task. Having finished her work ahead of time, she could see before her the perspective of an interminable Sunday extending to the end of time.

So, bit by bit it came about that she told herself she had been duped. She had believed she was making a gift of her law to the universe, but she had quite simply been sacrificing her own life. Never for a second had she taken the time to think of herself or her own beauty. She had made the wrong choice. She had been tricked, cheated. But why, indeed, why should she allow this state of affairs to go on? Already the revolt of an uneasy flame shone in her eyes. She examined her address books, studied herself in mirrors, inspected her wardrobe. Ruthlessly she judged her clothes and herself. Ruthlessly, but without false modesty, she finally decided to take advantage, and the best advantage possible, of a body, a face that had been unjustly neglected.

So then one fine morning she started making the rounds of hairdressers, beauty salons, milliners, dressmakers.

Her metamorphosis advanced at such a rate that at the end of a week a friend she had known that summer—one of the belvedere ladies—called to congratulate her on her daughter's approaching marriage and did not recognize her. She threw her corset to the winds, had her hair dyed yellow (the color of Petitdemange's beard) and cut very short, and used a jade cigarette-holder. And it was forbidden to call her "mother" or "grandmother" in the future. Everyone must address her as "Amie."

Finding it difficult to adapt to this new rule, the psychiatrist one evening, without doing so on purpose, reverted to his old habit of a third of a century and called her "my good woman," for which, despite his hoary locks, he was severely reprimanded.

"My good woman this, my good woman that . . ."

So well and so long did she mimic and ridicule him that the good man, despite his peaceful nature, ended by exploding:

"Is it senility, Madame, that is responsible for your losing all moral sense? What could be sadder than to see a woman of your age making a spectacle of herself by playing at being a little girl! You were the first to denounce Cynthia and her extravagant ways. But you, you yourself, I ask you, where do you expect to end up with those bare arms, that low neckline, as if you were always on the point of leaving for the Presidency Ball? As for your yellow hair . . ."

"My yellow hair," retorted Amie, "have you then forgotten the little you ever knew of worldly ways? All this harangue because I no longer dress as though I were a hundred. I am blonde, that's a fact. I don't deny it. I'm a blonde because it is my wish to be so. I had enough of the gray hairs that, thanks to you, I had before my time. When I think of the life you've given me for more than thirty years! Why did I never listen to my heart, my desires? I should have gone off in 1898 with the Persian prince, who, you remember, made such advances to me in Vichy. What eyes he had! It still makes me wild just to think of them. Eyes as big as saucers, and with what expression! He asked me to go off with him to Ispahan. Ispahan, the city of roses: '*The roses of Ispahan in their sheath of moss*.' This song was sung at the little party we gave in your honor when you were decorated. Right after the war. I felt the most horrible regret when I heard the singer from the *Opéra-Comique* evoking with his warm voice the Orient where I would have been adored as in a dream! But I thought of the brand-new red ribbon in your buttonhole. I wanted to be deaf, blind, to forget the magic world that I had renounced for you. For you, fool that I was. You might as well know, moreover, that the Persian prince was not the only one to speak tenderly to me. More than four men made flattering advances to me, and even, if you please, among your own colleagues, your friends. I was the beautiful wife, young, desirable, of a man who fell asleep as soon as his head touched the pillow. It cost me more than you will ever know to turn a stony profile and proudly oppose them. Each time I suppressed my feelings, I was a little more devoted to your name and to your work. To ward off temptation, I dressed in black. I called on old age and—why not admit it?—I called on death. Ah, learned sir, a bit less trigonometry and a bit more ardor and knowledge of the human soul! When I think it took me six times five years of monotonous martyrdom for me to get sick of you forever! Who else would have had my patience? At last the hour has come. I have yellow hair, as you so kindly point out. I have yellow hair, and if I feel so inclined, tomorrow it will be red, and green the day after . . ."

With that she left in high dudgeon. She slammed doors and retired to her own rooms. The positivist followed her, imploring her forgiveness. Without success. From her room the child could hear the reproaches that now lashed him. He was told that he had the blood of a turnip. Small wonder that his daughter could not hold her husband. Cynthia, whose failings, by the way, had been grossly exaggerated (still Amie speaking), Cynthia had certainly come out ahead. Would Petitdemange's betrothed be able to hold onto such an exemplary man? The worst was to be feared, with such a father. One schemed, worried, economized, worked like a dog. What good did it do? The best thing was to fall asleep so as to forget this mediocre life, this life without lyrical possibilities. But now, get a wiggle on, hit the hay. Good night.

"Good night, Amie," quavered a poor old voice.

On the other side of the partition, Amie tossed all night. Insomnia, or sleep that was scarcely any better; the next morning, an extra layer of makeup to repair her weary eyes and pallid cheeks. But after consulting the mirror, she no doubt feared that she might succumb to one of those more numerous, more ardent temptations, which her rediscovered youth could not fail to bring to life each day under her very footsteps; for, already as colorless of voice as she was freshly colorful of face (and in spite of her bared bosom, her naked arms that quivered with impatience as if they could no longer, even for a single minute, accept their wretched fate, she was still and forever resigned to monotony), yet that rejuvenated face offered twenty-to-one odds for escape, and she confided to the bride-to-be:

"Your father worries me. He is failing. You must get married quickly."

"Very well, Mother."

"Tonight Alfred and I will fix the exact date. The sooner the better. Otherwise . . ."

Otherwise . . . what did she mean by that otherwise . . . opening as it did on the terrifying unknown? Last evening she had been on the brink of defending Cynthia. Moreover, since she had selected this flamboyant mane, she was to a degree imitating the until now accursed English woman. She had not only copied the hairstyle of the goddess of the flaming helmet, but

also her gestures, her accent, her laugh. Cynthia, the object of horror and contempt, had become the model for an unexpected metamorphosis.

Otherwise . . . otherwise . . . hummed Amie. What in the world did she intend to convey by this *otherwise* . . . , which was as surely charged with threats as guns are with bullets? Against whom did she mean to use them? The temptation must have been very close at hand—indeed, very agreeably so—for Amie suddenly seemed about to yield to it, and, as if to stave off the evil desire, she concluded by repeating:

"Yes, tonight Alfred and I shall fix upon the exact date for the marriage."

But that evening at the customary hour, neither hair nor hide of Petitdemange was to be seen. He, who was always so punctual. Amie grew anxious, telephoned, retelephoned, to all the places where he might have been. To no avail. Time passed. Alfred did not arrive, could not be found.

"Oh dear, oh dear," wailed Amie.

"Cynthia may no longer be in Paris?" the grandfather suggested timidly.

"Cynthia, always Cynthia. Cynthia must be a nightmare to you. What do you mean to insinuate? You have the hypocrisy of all weaklings. Cynthia in Paris! Do you mean to say that Alfred, your daughter's fiancé and my best, my only friend . . . But have you taken a vow of insolence? Your remark is to me a direct and personal insult, do you understand, an ins—"

With impatience increasing her nervousness, and nervousness increasing her eloquence, Amie would doubtless have launched again into an entire tirade had not the telephone bell at that moment cut her short.

She stammered a "hello," rife with the anguish of the universe, and then, in torrents of fright came the rapid questions: "What? Wounded? Did you say 'wounded'? Seriously? At the Boucicaut Hospital? The heart has not been affected? The lungs? The liver? The stomach? Give me the details. I am a doctor's wife . . . Poor man! At least there's no danger of paralysis? I'm worried to death. Yes, yes, I am coming. Come, my child. You are his fiancée, after all. Alfred has been stabbed. Is the curse of heaven on our heads then?"

★
★ ★

The hospital.

In the room where they had put Petitdemange, everything was white on white. The one note of color, a beard whose fan lit up the fold of the sheet. A target, a bait, a talisman, this savage gold fascinated Amie.

"Alfred."

"Amie."

"Alfred. I am touching your beard, your mustache. Your heart is beating. I can feel it. You are alive. But how terrified I have been for you! My tenderness may be gauged by my anguish. So, dear Alfred, they wanted to kill you. Who is the monster, the guilty man?"

"The guilty woman. It was a woman, and a woman bolder than the greatest criminals of the classics. Her hands, like Lady Macbeth's, all the perfumes of Arabia . . ."

"Alfred, don't get so worked up. But what do you mean by Arabian perfumes? Is she a manicurist, a woman who sells scents, a hairdresser? Do explain . . ."

On the following day, when giving an account of her visit to the hospital, Amie began by admitting that she had at first feared a drama of passion. Imagine if Petitdemange had had a secret love affair! *Mais non*. But it must have been that his mind was wandering. The emotional shock had made him delirious. The nurse was unable to quiet him. So much the better, in one way, for what things he came up with!

Recalling Amie's dreams, had he not spoken of the owl-fish, and baptized her "his barometer of the beyond"? And with what diction! In spite of the fever, the sequence of his words was so perfect that, without exaggeration, there were moments when one could easily have believed one was at the Comédie Française, at a performance of *Andromaque*, for instance, when Pyrrhus begins his speech with the famous preamble:

Before all Greeks address you with my voice . . .

A touching and sublime evocation from a judge horizontal on his bed of pain, who spoke in a prose as fine as the late Mounet-Sully spoke in verse, his recitation of the trials he had undergone enough to wrench tears from even the hardest of hearts, for he had been faithful in his judicatory duty and to his promise to recover the bracelet of the Empress Eugénie's hair.

The bracelet of the Empress Eugénie's hair; for weeks and weeks now they had no longer spoken of it, but Petitdemange had not forgotten. Of all those involved in the affair, certainly not one of them could have imagined that a burglary several months old, like a commonplace apple tree that extends itself at nightfall in frightening shadows, might cast just as terrible menaces on the young fiancé's fate. And yet he had been all but assassinated. Had he been completely killed, the newly blonde, inconsolable lady knew that, despite the high quality of the hair dye, she would have instantly turned gray again. Fortunately (let us touch wood), the sister-phantom-owl-fish had not been mistaken in her happy prophecies. Great was the peril. That a man had been able to escape was enough to imply a miracle. A secret power watched over Petitdemange and, in protecting him, the entire family as well. In a week's time the assault that had almost cost the bearded mascot his life, his blond hair, and the finest of futures would fade into a simple memory. But what a scare all the same!

That very morning the Court of Justice had been informed of the arrest of Lucie, the little chambermaid, in a hotel in the Boulevard de la Chapelle, where, availing herself of the sleep of the young gardener, her lover who terrorized her, she had with a sure and inexorable hand planted a knife between his shoulder blades. A colleague of Petitdemange, who was in charge of the case, asked him, if he so wished, to be present at the reconstitution of the crime, which would take place on the premises in the course of the afternoon. Naturally, he was not going to miss such a fine opportunity. Here is a detailed description of the guilty woman as she appeared to Petitdemange: a wrinkled skirt, a gaudy and soiled blouse, an evil eye, cheeks vulgarly made up, the mouth not exactly red, but scarlet, violet, and so malleable her lips appeared to have been carved out of the lipstick she had painted them with.

This description once given, and with no fanciful touches (insisted the storyteller), was as faithful an account as possible of dear Alfred's testimony; and the psychiatrist, who was playing his last trumps, approved by an ad hoc diagnosis of the anger that suddenly swelled in Amie's throat and choked and strangled her. A glass of water had to be brought to her. The man of science took advantage of the interval. All gentleness, all discretion, he opined: "I understand your indignation. In the very room where she perpetrated her monstrous crime, that girl makes her appearance made-up. Thank you for your report. I shall make a note of this detail for my address to the Academy on kerosene fiends. Perverted taste. Perverted mind. Complete absence of moral feeling. The most dangerous kind of neuropath. Society must protect itself . . ."

"It is high time. If you had seen Alfred, as we did last night, on his bed of pain. The mere thought of it robs me of what strength I have. Another swallow of water. There, now I feel better. To continue: there was our fiancé among his colleagues. The subject under discussion was whether the accused had accomplices, for the victim had not only been lacerated by knife wounds, but there were also undeniable signs of strangulation. There was the slut, priding herself on having done this sinister work all alone. She claimed that nothing could be simpler, and if anybody were interested she could give a demonstration of how she set about it. Incidentally," remarked Amie, "every day of my life since my marriage I have heard it said that medicine is a priesthood that demands total renunciation. And the legal profession? Do you think your future son-in-law was not fully aware of the risk he was running when he offered to stretch out on the bed on the very spot where the gardener had been murdered? This did not prevent him from spreading himself flat on his stomach beside the murderess who seized him by the throat, and, *bang*, stuck him right in the middle of the back with the penknife that one of these gentlemen from the prosecutor's office had lent her to take the place of the fatal weapon. The blood began to flow. They rushed to his side. White as a sheet, Alfred attempted to lift himself up. Pain twisted his mouth, but he managed to summon enough strength to say: 'I am lost. Farewell, my friends. Say that I was happy to give my life for justice.' Whereupon, he collapsed. They thought he was dying, that he died a hero. Fortunately, the doctor from the law courts, who was attending the re-enactment, did not lose his head. The wounded man was taken to the hospital. As luck would have it, the wound was not too deep. He'll soon be well. But what a shock! If I had been there I would have strangled the little chambermaid with my own hands. At any rate, I hope she will receive the maximum. She certainly deserves it. Let us recapitulate. To sum up her crimes:

"Robbery.

"Blows and wounds. (This refers obviously to the tying up of the cook.)

"Murder.

"Attempt to murder a magistrate during the performance of his duty.

"The most she can hope for," concluded Amie, "is not to be guillotined, but she will surely be condemned to hard labor for life . . ."

The guillotine, hard labor for life. The child shuddered.

The blonder the grandmother grew, the more she decked herself out with baroque jewels, and the less one dared speak of Cynthia. Everyone was very happy that the drinker of kerosene had been found. Here at least was someone to jump on. And the grandfather, who called her a neuropath, spoke of her in terms he would not have used for a caterpillar or an earthworm. But how pretty she had been when she had sung the sad song of the *monte-en-l'air*! Her crimes? She had killed her lover. But he beat her. He was so strong, that boy, that sooner or later he would have ended up killing her. He was used to the earth, which never cries out when it is being martyrized. Digging had given him strong muscles. So when he hit he had

no idea of the consequences. "He terrorized her," the grandmother admitted to herself. He terrorized her. One night her
fear had been too much. On the table there was a knife. The
brute was asleep . . .

As to that attempted murder on the person of a magistrate
in the performance of his duties, one shouldn't exaggerate. In
any case, it served Petitdemange right. Moved by a despicable
curiosity, he had stretched himself out on a pallet of crime and
love. He had profaned the mystery of death and the mystery
of embraces. In contempt, a frail creature had made up her face
in such a rage that no sign of her true and touching counte-
nance could be discerned by the men of law. She had recognized one by one the coarse roses of the flowered wallpaper,
which, each morning on awakening, first met her eyes. She
remembered a song that spoke of prison and the scaffold. For
a minute she was tempted to hum it. It was at that moment she
was asked to demonstrate how she had set about . . . A shudder.
Since she had killed the one who had dominated her, why have
pity on any of those who belittled her grief, carrying insolence
to the point of pretending she was incapable of ridding herself
single-handed of that handsome lout she loved too well to leave,
to give up to another woman?

Little drinker of kerosene, you secretly sprinkled on your
handkerchiefs three drops of Cynthia's perfume, three drops
of happiness, though your teeth were clenched in despair, your
sly, murderous hands, even if drenched in liters and hundreds
of liters of rose-geranium, there would still be in your transparent nostrils the same obsession. Blood. Certainly not the
thin, insipid blood of Petitdemange. Your fingers, your palms,
your arms, your body and heart would not deign to be so much
as stained by it, not so much as marked by it. But that other

blood, that purple liquid of life that gave its strength, its odor, to his limbs, his torso, his face—to all that barbarous flesh against which your skin had liked to rub, that other blood, that warm fountain splashing upon a sleepless night, how could you forget it, the thick, dark blood of a husky fellow who, by taking you in his overpowering arms, by crushing you in an embrace of bone and rage, and by biting your neck, revealed to you the simple joy of fruit in the sun? You, little virgin, who ate thick slices of bread with mustard, and entwined the winter rains with the refrains of your despair. But the tears whose drops you no longer wiped away from your soft cheeks (as if believing they were the only possible dew in your life), did he not teach you how not to weep those tears, that king of the gardens who knew how to look straight into the single and gigantic eye of the August sky?

Boulevard de la Chapelle, where you showed a callous face. Petitdemange wounded, and you made no gesture, uttered not a word. You could have killed him and all his colleagues, one by one, and your lips would not have deigned to open to express a single regret. Nobility without pity for a creature handed over to the contemptible justice of men. Amie wanted to invent tortures, the grandfather stigmatized dope fiends and invoked the social weal; all voices were raised in a chorus of reproof, and yet what vertigo would have spun them, one and all, from the soil of their banality had they foreseen the abyss being dug deeper by each minute even in the presence of certain silences?

Little drinker of kerosene, they pelted you with horrible names. Cynthia, at the time of her major excommunication, was called a redhead, a whore. But you, they called you an infamous monster, a worthless slut, a *roulure*.*

*Translator's note: *Roulure*, a slang word for prostitute, is used throughout this passage as a literal derivative from the verb *rouler*, to roll.

Roulure: before the globe attained its desired rotundity, much labor was expended on shaping it, and tests made to polish it. Sad shavings of elements and beings were scattered to the four corners of the heavens in order that the terrestrial curve be made more even, more perfect, pathetic rubbish was widely dispersed: the peelings of cosmogony, the wind, the rain, and the fire of heaven, later to be reassembled in one whirling gesture and petrified in the surrounding ether. Thus joined and fused, they fell to earth again, waste matter that only the miracle of tempests on high, higher even than the menagerie of clouds, would blend in the most brilliant resurrection. *Roulure*, this word so viscid, so ugly on family tongues, was purified, ignited, illuminated, gilded childhood dreams, and rolled in the sun. *Roulure*, pretty girl whom nothing human could restrain, *roulure*, O, beautiful silent one! Never in all her life would a little child forget the song of the *monte-en-l'air*, nor could she ever forgive a certain examining magistrate for pretending to be assassinated, whereas, under the pretext of convalescence, he had been installed in the best bedroom in the house, the one where Cynthia had lived for weeks and weeks among flowers, frocks, valises abloom with the names of strangely lettered palaces, and perfume bottles of mystery and dreams. Cynthia, who was a whore like death, and the little kerosene drinker, who was a *roulure*, certainly could not be loved by those inured only to banality and gloom. But the dung of insults opened the way to the springing to life of a glorious flowering. One might try to desecrate them, but nothing could sully these amorous women. Nevertheless, this did not prevent the little girl from holding a grudge against the man who had taken the place of the red-haired goddess, and whose praises were now sung by the entire household. Amie had discovered that he was the world's most celebrated judge. A bit of good news that the cook lost no time in spreading everywhere in the servants' stairway. She explained: "The fiancé of these ladies, well, every woman is wild about him. Mobs of actresses, singers, middle-class women, marquises, and princesses he's never set eye on, and whom he couldn't tell from Adam and Eve, send him proposals by the kilo. It's been sad in our house since the first Monsieur went off. But there's no question about the happiness today."

"Yes, but there's the reverse side of the medal," escaped from Amie in a sigh one day.

Already her anxieties had become more specific. Had it not been decided that the bride and groom would go to the Canary Islands for their honeymoon? But the sun has never agreed with the bride, and whenever she is out in the open her skin begins to smart, burn . . . Having departed with a colorless wife, Petitdemange would come back with a lobster.

And Amie, however, would never cease to grow younger.

Out in the open air, facing the sun from three o'clock of a winter's afternoon, and from four to five of the intermediary seasons (spring and autumn) until six in summer on one hand and on the other, at whatever hour of day in the house, thanks to the soothing aid of the wisely chosen ochre tulle curtains— she knew that her new hairdo, her earrings, topaz balls engraved with the signs of the zodiac, her clever gowns, her drooping-brimmed hats, the artful use of cosmetics, the discreet support of a brassiere, endowed her with a face and figure capable of attracting attention and, what was more important, worthy of holding it . . .

And the perfume—not such a perfume as Cynthia's, which could be perceived only if one pressed one's nostrils to her skin.

If one uses scent, at least let it smell, declared Amie judiciously, and she sprayed her bare arms with a daring concoction. Thus Petitdemange prolonged his hand kisses of greeting. His lips slowly learned to follow the path that led to the bend of the arm, to that delicate oasis that quivers so deliciously when surprised by a beard, a mustache.

"Stop, stop!" begged Amie.

"My head is turning. Your perfume intoxicates me. What is its name?"

"It is a blend of *Tenderness* and *Eternal Desire*."

". . . . . . ."

". . . . . . ."

A blend of *Tenderness* and *Eternal Desire*.

Who indeed would not allow himself to be captured by such snares? Perfumes?

Amie, Petitdemange, motionless on a sofa, dream on of the secrets of your preposterous triangular bellies and your hexagonal hips. You have been decapitated of the diamond stopper that serves you as head, and suddenly it is the miracle of freshly shaven armpits. To think that the thick hair that had until now been allowed to grow freely there, year after year, had known no intimacies save those of the dreariest of almond soap. What wasted time. A blend of *Tenderness* and *Eternal Desire*. Two beings asked only to be swept away in a mutual and whirling ecstasy. But their proud souls feared the superficiality of such attempts at love, frozen in silence, the renunciation. Petitdemange, with his matchless beard, resembled the Assyrian colossi. Amie, still striving to resist her overwhelming passion, clutched at words.

"I am your future mother-in-law. The invitations were delivered this very morning, and in a week's time, at this hour, at the town hall of the sixteenth arrondissement . . ."

"In eight days at this very hour at the town hall of the six-teenth . . ."

"Exactly as I said, in eight days at this very hour at the town hall of the sixteenth . . ."

"Too bad!" cried Petitdemange, who could take no more.

And suddenly a wife who had never kissed any other man save her psychiatrist, discovered that positivists, decidedly, did it very badly indeed. In her mouth, on her tongue was another tongue, which she sucked like the candy-sticks of childhood. A lover, I have a lover, she was thinking . . . Heedless of every-thing, of scandal even, she never dreamed of moving, although the door was opening. Petitdemange remembered a little late the inconveniences of being caught in *flagrante delicto*, and had difficulty in extricating himself, while Amie, fearing to lose the memory of that strange saliva in her jaws, remained at least five minutes without speaking in the presence of her daughter, as blanched and mute as she herself.

Finally recovered, she declared:

"Destiny. We were wrong to fight against it. My child, your happiness lies elsewhere. It was I, you remember, who was vis-ited by the portentous fish . . . No one can defy fate . . ."

★
★ ★

Neither Petitdemange nor Amie made an appearance at din-ner.

The child was told that they had gone on a journey.

"Like Papa and Cynthia?" she asked.

The next day, she heard the cook explaining it to the servants from the apartment house:

"This family—it's like butter in the frying pan. It melts so fast that maybe there'll soon be nobody but me standing there all alone in front of my stove. The women are always going off with the men they shouldn't. And the young one, she's left in the lurch. Well, that's life, my friends. It's life. It's love. Come back, I'll keep you up to date."

CHAPTER FIVE

The Child Becomes a Woman

A postal card with a view of the pyramids bore Amie's Egyptian greetings.

"I have news of grandmother. She has written me from the banks of the Nile. She went to see the Sphinx."

"... the banks of the Nile, the Sphinx," repeated a man indifferent to these fathomless dreams, to the enigmatic monster, a man too involved in the sciences to be distracted by the illusionary dream of travel, or by the prestige of a river, or of some legendary beast.

It was of little importance to him, a continent trod by guilty feet, as a faithless woman and her accomplice traveled around the globe. From now on, a seeker sheltered from words, from scowls and glances that threatened to destroy his faith, he had taken up his work again, happy to know that never again would his efforts be ridiculed nor his discoveries scoffed at. What remained of his life would be consecrated to perfecting his theory of mushroom-acts, and the gravity of such labors, also their subtleties, and the many hypotheses and deductions would leave no time to curse an adulterous woman. Let her jump with both feet across the equator, cross deserts on camelback, bathe in every ocean of the world, she would run no risk of being stoned to death. The positivist had not the slightest desire to cast so much as a tiny pebble at her. Furthermore, because severe discipline safeguarded him from passionate exaggerations, he did not feel that the right of pardon lay with him.

Did he have a grudge against the sea because of its tides, the sky for its storms?

A sixty-year-old woman, having cast her stays to the wind, had gone to the Sphinx in quest of some of those enigmas for which her sister owl-fish had given her a dangerous taste. Exultant at having abducted her own daughter's fiancé and dyed yellow her mutilated locks, drunk with a newly achieved freedom, there she was in the land of the Pharaohs; but a psychiatrist who was not to be deceived by the romanticism of appearances looked down from the heights of his serene wisdom, as if from a lighthouse where, despite the anger of the clouds, the howls of the wind, and the tumult of the waters, the grandiloquent play of the tempests appeared extremely simple, and he knew full well that this tardy sinner had only obeyed those natural laws that determine the fate of human beings in spite of themselves.

"Senile nymphomania," diagnosed this scrupulous observer. Besides, alas, this was not such a rare malady. Demon of the noon of life. "Noon to two o'clock," he smiled—an innocent revenge—for with tranquillity he had recovered that dry wit that the fugitive herself had in other days been fond of praising. But if it were a case of senile nymphomania, that is a morbid psychosis, and perhaps even with some organic injuries, one would have to be without a sense of justice should one dare condemn, or fly into a rage, or seek vengeance, demand, for instance, in the name of reprisal, a divorce . . . And which of the two, in reality, was the more ridiculous, the more to be pitied. a scholar whose career had been heaped with honors, or a magistrate who had ruined his future by packing himself off, bag and baggage, to follow through exotic countries an old, peroxided blonde?

Since the evening he was told of the flight of Petitdemange and the woman he had for more than thirty years called his life mate, this reasonable man, instead of crying out, and moaning, or clenching his fists, lost not one whit of his serenity, but, happy to be rid of her so cheaply, requested that he be allowed the time for a thorough examination of the facts. Closed in his study, he had remained three hours lost in reflection. His daughter and granddaughter waited for him in silence in the large *salon.* When he came to join them, the woman made a sign that the child should leave. But he, in one word, expressed his wish to the contrary, convinced that it would be marvelously instructive, this still warm example from which it was so easy to draw conclusions highly suitable to the formation of a youthful mind. And off the bat he began:

"The distressing spectacle of catastrophes due to daydreaming and a taste for the vague and mystic unknown has converted intelligent people to the cult of those two rulers of the Universe: Reason and Observation. By them alone can we attain a knowledge of reality. This knowledge is not always flattering to our human pride. But the delights of falsehood, of artificial paradises, conceal many other pitfalls. Here we are this evening come together to deplore very sad events. And you, my daughter, even more than I, are to be pitied. But my duty as man and positivist is to help you to see as clearly as possible, even though at the cost of great suffering, into all this imbroglio. The diagnosis established, we can look for the remedy. Should I confess to you that I believe I know it? In a few days you will be happy again, and this time for life, my child. But let us not anticipate things. To recapitulate: two women of your family, one your own mother, have each of them in the space of a few months robbed you of two men who had each pledged you eternal faith. This is neither the time nor the place to make an apology for Cynthia. Just the same, though I never allowed myself to be affected by it, I can understand how seductive, if it came to that, this handsome auburn-haired creature might be; but your mother? As if I were to start playing the gigolo! However, she and Petitdemange are having a perfect romance. It would be a farce were it not a tragedy. Who could have foreseen such a denouement? It is true that the sciences of the soul, insubordinate as they are to facts, are still in an embryonic state. A paradox of our civilization. One must submit to an examination to have the right to drive a car, and yet any empty dream whatsoever claims with impunity the full and entire liberty of the emotional life. Thus it is that creatures who are actual social menaces can, without hindrance, exercise their fatal talents. Because of them, the most respectable homes are metamorphosed into Babylon and the least prophylactic rendered impossible. Under my roof, under my very nose and beard, opium has been smoked, kerosene been drunk, and a hitherto upright magistrate has been debauched. But harm once done is over with, and since we are rid of Cynthia and my wife, the problem is to prevent them from returning and frustrating you again. This much decided, let us consider your possibilities for happiness. You have inherited my stable nature. Therefore you must make a home again, and as quickly as possible. Experience has cured us of the superstition of so-called irreproachable men of the world. And so if, as I have already observed, harm once done is no longer to be done, that which has not been done is still to be done. This means that we should not exaggerate the guarantees of a blameless past but, on the contrary, consider the promises of a future that, if not perfect, will at least be consistent with the consequences of former errors, and will cure forever those who made them of any desire to begin them again. So, after deep reflection, I have decided that for you the best thing is to marry a certain penitent of my acquaintance. A missionary who, not satisfied with his task as evangelist, teaches the benefits of positivistic wisdom to the savages of Africa, the underworld of Europe. The Society for Protection by Rational Experience has listened many times to his reports with the greatest interest and with the greatest profit. Of British origin, this reverend gentleman is called Mac-Louf . . ."

"Mac-Louf?"

"Yes, Mac-Louf. This name may be less pleasing to French ears than La Rochefoucauld or Talleyrand-Périgord, but the gratification that men derive from three or four syllables that call the attention of their contemporaries to them, we know what it is worth. The pride of calling oneself Countess of X, or Baroness of Z—what vanity compared to a respectable peace."

"Undoubtedly, Father."

"So you raise no objection to this marriage?"

"No, Father . . ."

"That's good. I am indeed happy. But so that you may not be surprised when you see him for the first time, I must tell you that Mac-Louf is not exactly a giant. He is not quite five feet tall. But if he is short, he has been clever enough to make the most of it. Of an excellent family, but orphaned at the age of six months, Mac-Louf had to provide for himself at a very early age, and here I will allow myself to remark in passing that the school of hard knocks is still the best teacher. In turn groom, magician, sacristan, botanist, the poor fellow, finding himself one day without work, attached a cardboard hump to his shoulders to keep himself from dying of starvation. He filled his hump with narcotics, which he sold wherever he could. Thus for three years he traveled all over the world with a whole selection of drugs on his back. He was so small that his gibbosity caused no surprise. But one day, as bad luck would have it, his hump, inadequately fastened, started to bounce up and down as he was going through customs at Vintimiglia. The fraud was discovered. Condemned to several months in prison, Mac-Louf had time to meditate. He had paid a price to learn whither leads an existence outside the law. His sentence served, he betook himself to the central office of the Evangelical Missions in Marseilles. As during his humpback days he had frequented outlaws, and as he was familiar with the freemasonry of the slums, he was very quickly put in charge of the preaching in slang in the ports. He went to music halls, to bawdy houses, and in the words these strayed sheep themselves use, he expounded on the Gospel and spoke of the realities of life. His orations had nothing to do with vulgar and ludicrous nonsense. The Society for Protection by Rational Experience and the Positivist League delegated a certain authority to him. That is to

say, he is not a mere nobody. Shall I invite him to lunch tomorrow?"

"Yes, Father."

★

★ ★

The next day, when she came back from classes, the little girl
heard the cook recounting the events of the day for the benefit
of the servants of the apartment house.

"What a commotion, my friends! First of all this morning I
was called to take the duds of the old lady to Petitdemange's
house. She came to the door herself, dolled up like an old co-
cotte in pink silk pajamas. A lady who up to a few months ago
was still wearing the nightgowns from her trousseau, simple
nightgowns with a bit of scalloping around the neck. She
brought me into a room where the judge was taking it easy in
the middle of the bed that should have been his wedding bed
with her daughter. Talk of a shock! Completely shattered, I
came back home. Hardly had I put foot in the door when, bang,
the old fellow comes into my kitchen. He totters in, but for all
that he has a cool head on his shoulders. A great scientist they
say he is, but it was himself in person who ordered the menu.
A fine lunch. It seems he had invited a big shot. At one o'clock,
the bell rings. The valet who went to open the door came back
twisted like a corkscrew, my friends, enough to make you believe he was suffering from a miserable attack of colic. But, my
eye! It was just that he was laughing, a fit of laughing that was
contorting him as though he would be screwed up like a but-
tonhook for the rest of his life. At last, when he could speak
again, he told me:

" 'They've invited a dwarf!'

" 'A dwarf?' was what I came back with.

"And since he told me it wasn't every day that one had the chance of seeing such a shrimp of a creature, I went to get a squint at him myself. I see an abortion, tall as a cabbage, fat as a rat, dressed in black. Something like a revivalist. And guess what? This twisted creature is going to marry the young lady . . ."

★

★ ★

"Three whisks of a lamb's tail and it was done," the cook was to state the very day after Mac-Louf's and the mother's wedding. "And now, off traveling they go! The old woman is with the Bedouins, and our newlyweds are off to India. This one-yard-square husband, he crosses an ocean the way we go to Saint-Cloud. Everyone has the moving mania. Lady Cynthia and her lover are somewhere in the Americas. The old man and the kid are the only ones to stay put . . ."

There they stayed. While three couples went around the world. The father and Cynthia, so as not to be sullied by routine, that moss whose sad greenness spreads on quiescent bodies and hearts; Petitdemange and Amie, because they wished to embellish their love, walked hand in hand upon the slopes of the Himalayas, questioning the Tibetan llamas, shivering among the enigmatic ruins of Asia, prayed on the Acropolis, crawled on all fours through virgin forests, cooked themselves in the Palm Beach sun, and still found time to ask fortunetellers in all the European capitals when, finally, would the death of an old man, who obstinately refused a divorce, allow them to wed properly; in Africa, Mac-Louf and the mother were busy converting Negroes.

All of them had contemplated Niagara Falls, the stable wherein Christ was born, and the drolly coiffed Chinese cities. Their feet had trod soil where the grass could be seen growing right before their eyes, while a little girl lived in her drab Europe, watching time slip by. Time . . . a peculiar river. The days, the years, slavish tributaries flow into the shapeless mass that comes from no one knows where. An indifferent shipwreck. The monotonous waters rise. After attempting a song, a child could not capture even a few drops to quench her thirst. At the highest peak of the cruel blue sky gleamed a metal orb that seared the earth. Steel, whose light cuts, splits, and stabs. For, having lorded it over the trees, as in the days of red balloons, the beaten gold suddenly fell crumpled, dying, on the lawns, and the slaughtered clouds no longer appeared to searching eyes to be a flock browsing between heaven and earth, herded by that invisible shepherd, the wind. Rags of misery, poor faded things, tatters hung on the nails of the stars, the shadows they cast on the early years were fabulous gulfs opening onto the horizontal ennui of days, never to bloom again. In the too white, too crude glare, exhausted hope turned to dust. How could feet leave their imprint on this desert? Legs that disdained to stagger through the marsh of petty hatreds, hands that would not condescend to rummage through the sordid debris of hours, a breast that felt the swelling of the heart and wished to reach out, breathless and defenseless, toward that angle of stones that causes all springs to gush forth anew, spirit too proud ever to accept serving as a receptacle for the drops of memory, O, you, child becoming a woman, you would not deign to stoop and gather the accessible flowers and the deceptive foliage that the habitual cowardice of man tries to make into a bouquet, nothing more of your past will be able to hold you back! But where are the great wild beasts, rank and magnificent, whose cries seem made of sun? And how to erect marble forests for them on this dust? At night, gigantic serpents of jade, who would perish rather than become servile again, stand erect, bearing upon their minuscule ruby heads a dome composed of Cynthia's colors: russet, white, and green. At dawn they crystallize into trees of salt, melt, and only small black stains remain to remind men of their existence. Memory is the ink that corrupts all flesh, all splendor. In the grandfather's library there was a very curious book on tattooing. The child becoming a woman knew with what designs the pretty-lipped sailors stained the innocence of their chests, and, in order to get the better of time and forgetfulness, scoffed at the vigorous pursuit of sex. And there is no acid that is able to restore purity to an epidermis so despoiled. Memory, the tattooing with which the weak, the betrayed, the exiled, believe they have armored themselves. Scarcely has the sentimental garland succeeded in knotting itself around one arm than the heart turns to another love. The father and Cynthia had never felt the need to write something on their skins. Likewise, they condemned all that human beings surround themselves with in the belief that they are protecting themselves, their destinies. In no corner of the earth were there customs, or a house, or furniture, they could share in common. No testimony of their passion would remain to cause remorse or regrets. And yet, parallel vagabonds, who had never asked anything of each other, promised nothing, they had loved each other for months, for years, each day a little more.

Contrary to this, the young woman who had taken a thousand precautions, who had believed she was protected by legal handrails, had twice in a row been abandoned. And here she

was reduced to following a missionary dwarf to the country of
wild beasts. She who was afraid of the simple wasps of the Ile-
de-France now slept in a hut of rushes roofed with leaves, from
which could be heard at night, all hot and menacing, the dance
of the panthers who are never sleepy. So in the terror of her
dreams shone chaplets of feline eyes. Nightmares the color of
sulphur, dreams rent by the striking of great claws, and, at long
last, the dawn. From her palliasse she contemplated the pious
Mac-Louf asleep, lying on his back, his hands clasped. The
apostolic flesh of this husband one yard square (as the cook
described him) would surely be no temptation to the cannibalistic Negroes should they be inclined to add a little human
touch to their menu. It would be the young woman who would
be turned on the spit. Decidedly, early morning in Africa holds
little comfort for newlyweds. Arise, most holy Mac-Louf, dis-
card that long, that puritanical nightgown that makes you look
like an oldish and parchmented angel. But how soundly you
sleep now that you are no longer haunted by the fear of the
police and customs. They restored your peace of mind when
they confiscated your cardboard hump. And you let pass the
hour for caresses. That of prayer has now rung. Up, reverend
sir, you must get up. Kisses on the forehead, and then a young
couple in nightshirts kneel down to ask the blessing of the
Almighty. Following that, a screen is unfolded. Gentlemen on
one side, ladies on the other, and discreet ablutions get under
way. When she has finished brushing her teeth, Mrs. Mac-Louf
begs her husband to invite, under threat of hellfire, the catechumens to the mission. Then, this evening, they would perhaps bring up an extra pitcher of water from the river in which
one dared not bathe for fear of crocodiles, hippopotami, and
other gentle animals. Once they have washed, the screen is

folded again. Mac-Louf appears with a black necktie, impeccable in his alpaca redingote. He drinks his tea and then, Bible in hand, leaves the hut. Outside, he opens a parasol lined with green. He walks between the bizarre huts of this primitive village, and he is moved, for every door opens as he passes and his flock follows him as chickens collect behind servant-girls in the hope of being fed. Spiritual food, he thinks tenderly. But here we are already in the main square where nourishment for the soul is dispensed. Giants, insolently nude, squat around the small, clothed man. Some eat bananas, others bare their fine cannibalistic teeth. "Dust, thou are but dust," warns Mac-Louf, and the catechumens, to contradict him, deal one another hearty slaps. "Dust, thou art but dust." The din of bare palms, the nervous tom-tom of bellies, drowns out the preacher's tiresome oratory. But in the resonant bodies, the game threatens to become a little less innocent.

Mac-Louf, parched of all desire by the heat, left to their temptations a people who knew no other clothing than rings in the nose. In the high grasses, there was a fricassee of thighs. Rosy desires within black wool were details that the bearer of the good word preferred to ignore. He returned to his hut where his bride was mending the linen. A light lunch. The afternoon was devoted to drawing up reports. Europe must be made aware of all the troubles caused by these niggers who grow even faster than the gigantic plants and monstrous trees of their land. At nine years of age, they are men and women. And their intelligence hasn't the leisure for a parallel development. Hence the precarious position of their civilization, the indecency of their morals, the absurd character of their actions, which might all be classified in the famous category of mushroom-acts. The missionary was a genius at official communi-

cations. He was also a first-class letter writer. Thus his letters, even his smallest cards, were manna from heaven to a Parisian psychiatrist. And so many reflections on the method of organizing a continent where it is no rarity to meet mothers ten or eleven years old. Happy little pickaninnies, naked in the noontime African sun. Indulge yourselves to your heart's content on your mattresses of tropical grasses, while the preacher writes to his old marionette of a father-in-law, deploring in his finest style your sexual precocity. A child becoming a woman learned to hate the straight streets of cities and well-built houses where life passes by as one merely waits. That bosom with its two little breasts, very small, but two real small breasts, which no one had as yet wanted to caress. If we were in Négrerie,* no one would have ignored this tender fruit. Young boys with slender legs would have turned to smile. One of them, encountered by chance, would have so successfully persisted with teeth and eyes that a new young body would have succumbed to the urgency of long black fingers. Negro hands, your palms fresher than open pomegranates, what temptation for a young girl who dreamed of love as spring dreams of fruit! Let lilac-time merge with the season of peaches, let continents mingle as well, overdressed Europe, and Africa without so much as a loincloth. The child becoming a woman fell in love. At first she did not know with whom, but soon she came to know it was with a colored boy. She loved him. She had seen his portrait. He was called "Le Nègre." The eighteenth century had already foreseen him. La Tour had painted his face, his bust. He had clothed him. But under the muslin of his shirt, the rose velvet of his coat, it was easy to guess into what shoulders the neck curved. The head was in three-quarter view. A topaz elongated

*Translator's note: This is a place where Negroes are confined for the slave traffic.

the one visible ear. The eyes were sad because of this exile in a frame, in the very heart of a drab town. Every day of the fortnight that she had to stay in Geneva with her grandfather, who had come there to follow the activities of a commission on the international prohibition of drugs (Cynthia, beware—but when was there to be an international prohibition of mushroom-acts?), the little virgin went to see "Le Nègre." Once her visit was made, she would lean above the waters of the lake so as not to lose the mauve and maroon memory of his face. Had "Le Nègre" been able to leave the flat prison of the canvas, he would surely have unhesitatingly cast the hypocrisy of the jacket and shirt to the four winds from the bridge of the Rhone. And what a plunge he would have taken into that cold and emerald torrent, his muscles challenging its treacheries. Reborn from the foam, he would have gone with the child becoming a woman to a garden of actual trees and lovely hind. Alas, one recovers from puerility as from an illness, with an aching of dreams and growing pains. Sad in his rose velvet on a background of pastel blue, there, in Geneva, the Negro remained. According to Mac-Louf, his sister, the Negress, had been a mother since the age of eleven. Therefore she had known love.

While the psychiatrist obstinately talked on and on about every hygiene, the physical, the spiritual, the social, the child becoming a woman wanted to tear to shreds the everlasting curtain of his speech that hung between her anxiety and the stage where the true comedy, the true drama, would be played.

At last, the miracle: a little colored girl was sent by the missionary from the Congo to help the cook, who was growing old. Of the two adolescents, the one who could decline regular Greek verbs found herself to be the illiterate one, for the other, in words of one syllable, judged life and its joys and tribulations, and knew by experience, and truly, how sweet to young breasts were the thick lips of the boys of her own land. Blue shade of the palms, the oasis of noon, what games were played with little black tits, nibbled, squeezed, by impatient fingers to make the pulp burst from the hard, cold fruit.

"Yes, but at twenty," interrupted the pushy and all too prescient chambermaid who had replaced the drinker of kerosene, "at twenty their breasts, little one, wobble this way and that."

"Wobble this way and wobble that. That's funny," said the little Negress, showing all her teeth.

"That depends, my dear," retorted the pretentious skivvy. "I have an uncle who was adjutant in Senegal. He says that the women of twenty down there can throw their paps over their shoulders, pass them under their arms, and bring the nipples back in front again. An old tire, that's what a Negress's breast is like. You think that's funny?"

"Me, the hell I care."

But already there was no longer any way to drag a word out of Bamboula. Her white eyes scorned the resinous pine of the linen room and returned in longing to a country planted with muscular thighs, with carnal trees, whose leaves are hands, tough and skillful in their caresses. Wobble this way and wobble that. On the zinc roofs of Europe fell a rain that rotted espadrilles, a rain whose traitorous complaint accompanied in even greater despair the song of the *monte-en-l'air*.

Down there in Africa, great, hot, bruising drops revive all the colors, restore a green, varnished youth to plants gray with fatigue, and render the grasses more welcoming to the loves of the morrow. As for the old world, you can water it all you want but nothing grows there any more. Cities of iron and hearts of stone, everything is built without song. Not a stick of wood is visible in all this masonry; in the ossified squares, no vegetal surprise. One street only in Paris allows dandelions to grow between its cobblestones. It is no less lost in this century, nor stranger to its customs, nor ready to be offended concerning them, than was in his day the man who gives the street his name. It is called Agrippa d'Aubigné. Now in the rue Agrippa d'Aubigné, in 1927, it was easy to forget the boredom of positivism, the bearded felony of magistrates, and the hideousness of missionaries. There was enough here to decide the child becoming a woman and the little Negress to choose to linger on one afternoon when a certain young whistling workman persisted in following them. This handsome insolent youth was capable of withstanding the insistence of twice two eyes. A cap was raised, a lock slipped down. An apprentice of the faubourgs wore a smile on his lips as young Arabs a flower in the corner of their mouths. Two hearts felt their bosoms tighten. The young girls trembled. It was not with fear. The sun recovered its confidence and illuminated the infinite promise of the blue on high, so very high, and despite the gritty crusher of life from the soil, a corolla of yellow restored the true earth that was sweet to tread. The child becoming a woman blushed, for she thought that under his canvas jacket, which did not permit a stitch of underwear to be seen, the man who dared to stare at her was perhaps nude. But we are always naked under something, she suddenly realized. The Negro in Geneva was nude under his old rose velvet, like his unbanished brothers under the simple, the dazzling, heat of the day. Naked, there is happiness only for bodies liberated from their clothes. And now, from the *côte d'azur* of his adolescence, was the whistling laborer about to produce, as if from the waters, the god of the sea? Here would be the most miraculous of beaches, but if she touched even with the tip of a finger this boy whom she had not known that morning, how could she dare to go on living? And the grass would blush between the cobblestones of dear rue Agrippa d'Aubigné. The European girl was ashamed. But not the little savage who approached him, walking on the tips of her toes so that her teeth might knock against the whistler's teeth. Already pressed to a body that the impatience of small fingers tested for desire, the better to recall the breast, the belly, the thighs of her playmates in the full sunlight of African noons, she closed her eyes and a wave swept her back to the land of giant immodesties, of tropical rains, of love.

The child becoming a woman leaned against a wall and wept.

She loathed the rue Agrippa d'Aubigné, Negresses, hooligans, and the entire world.

CHAPTER SIX

The City
of Flesh

Their mission accomplished, the Mac-Loufs sailed the sea of
return.

And that same week, in the same port, two other couples
were due to arrive: the father and Cynthia, Petitdemange and
Amie. Thus it became a question of killing three birds with a
single stone. The psychiatrist, who had decided to go and meet
the Mac-Loufs, would take his granddaughter with him so that
she might greet those whose conduct had not been as circumspect as it should have been yet who were, nonetheless, her
family. The little Negress would also be included in the trip,
for now that she was willing to deck herself out as an Anglo-
Saxon maid, it was only fitting that she be seen as a living
example by the side of the converter who had had such trouble
persuading her to be so good as to wear a chemise the day he
sent her off from Africa to Europe.

Farewell to the armchair of dreams, where in childhood the smile of a beautiful, auburn-haired Englishwoman had shone brightly across the oceans, and then, at a less puerile age, the gaze so tenderly sad of the Negro in pastel rose, and, finally, the first real temptation within hand's reach, the fine insolence of the young laborer about whom, despite the longing to hear him spoken of, she could never bring herself to ask the wild child for the slightest bit of news.

She who was becoming a woman had until then been condemned to such a restricted life that she felt herself already another person at the thought of leaving for a Mediterranean port. Her former life in the house where Cynthia smoked opium, a future criminal drank kerosene, Amie debauched Petit-demange, a scientist put his finishing touches on his theory of mushroom-acts, and a young, scarcely nubile girl from the Congo described the moments and joys of love as a European might give an account of a tea party or an afternoon at the cinema—all this past she left behind to go meet three traveling couples, knowing that she would find none of it, and wanted to find none of it, on her return.

Railway cars moving along rails, your wheels are not so artlessly round as one might like to believe. The heavy ebb and flow of your cast-iron refrains in the fragile night, alone, under the shadow of eyelids of blue cloth, protect the twinkling and watchful eye of the gas flame, and the unyielding rhythm of your vagabond hope, and the interval between a jolt and a harsh resumption of this refrain, your times of rest, such are the true songs of departure. Like a mist on your inexorable rhythm is the frail breathing of sleeping creatures. The positivist, sedately stretched the full length of his bench, snored in short, regular blasts. The Negress laughed in her dreams, and the child becoming a woman, between waking and sleeping, between earth and sky, listened to time drawing away, but could not imagine which couplets would be accurately scanned by this train as it pitched headlong into the tunnels of the future.

She no longer knew anything, but remained incapable of foreseeing what was to come.

The dark womb of the night was later to give rebirth to the Negro, his one visible ear elongated by a topaz. He was called Future. He had thrown away through the train door the rococo clothes in which they had rigged him out. From his share of travelers, he would choose the one most worthy of his muscles, of his lisping melancholia, and of his topaz earring. Already his hand lightly touched the nape of a neck. But his older sister, Negro as well, named Memory, became jealous (for, according to Mac-Louf, incest was an everyday occurrence in Africa) and with her traitorous hands she squeezed a mauve and maroon throat. Future was thus assassinated in silence, the Negro body was hurled into the passing night with scarcely a sound, scarcely a mark. No one would ever know of Memory's crime. Her limbs were so nimble that not even a speed of 100 kilometers an hour prevented her from jumping lightly down on the track. Free in the dawn, she laughed at the sight of that serpent of steel and iron rushing headlong into nothingness. To add to her joy, she rubbed the virgin black of the tips of her breasts with open palms, accompanying this rotary motion with words, difficult to translate:

Ho la rio to atcho palaïo
Aïo la mio vokno Rotadcho
Digo mugo rudou banaïou.

All the weight of her crime and of her body rested on the toe of one foot as she went on spinning tiptoes to the cemetery. There she fashioned a bouquet from the beaded flowers that grow on tombs. How startling, this figure of inexorable onyx wreathed in the vegetation of mourning! Your arms heavy with giant pansies, with palms of crudest green, you chirruped, shoeblacked dove. The attire that widows reserve for the houses of dead men went well with your skin. Between your breasts you pinned a violet stain and, following its initial reflection, an entire rainbow took fire from your polished belly. But what was this wild animal disguised as a whistling young laborer seeking in the shivering dawn? Handsome brute, the cunning of the faubourgs made you a bewitcher of Negresses. On the stone that reminds the living of the completed existence of who knows which Dupont, it was easy to bed with the flower girl of the past. Tit and Tat. And to enjoy to the point of howling aloud a flower sweeter by far to the membrane of the male than all the others so humbly vegetable, or even those called flowers of memory. But, cocky youth, you took your leave without so much as awaking the dozing Negress with a triumphant shout. Much as she might stretch herself wide for other rapes, she would have to leave before the gravediggers arrived.

She left, and the brooks she passed revealed to her that the seducer who had taken her between a tombstone and his desire had stamped the corpses' names in letters of dust on her nudity. You scorned the refreshing shock of rivers, for on your skin was something that could not be effaced. But, tell me, you whose black triumph was already fading to gray, do you believe that endives bleaching in cellars care to remember the sun? As civilized infants are born knowing how to whimper, you were born knowing how to swim, but because the water whose sprite you were knows no respect for the minute that is eternalized by a powdering of dust, even your weary feet wanted no more of the cool relief streaming all over you in the days when you had nothing left to remember. And all this trouble for the pride of wearing a skewer across your back, a diagonal supplication beginning at the west buttock and terminating east of the nape of the neck, recommending:

Pray for him.

Him? Who? Him? The faceless wanderer who struck forests of sparks from a slab of marble? The blue canvas bird of prey or the bird of blood that the hooligan of rue Agrippa d'Aubigné called: Maidenhead.

"Do you have your maidenhead, Mademoiselle?"

Such is the question loafing novices ask in the springtime, after one of those songs that make a gift of their optimism to carpenters all over the world. The child becoming a woman did not answer this question. She fled, eyes burning with tears like those Iphigenia shed in despair at having to die without ever knowing love. Those who die virgin do not rot, it is said. The embalmer is chastity, the trains, the night, are the mosaics of solitary slumber. Of all the travelers, there was not one who had not closed his heart with a key. Bodies shook this way and that against each other, but never for a second were aroused by even the most furtive sensuality. And what if they remained wedged in their corners for eternity, with, by way of a halo, the three prophetic letters: P.L.M.—*Pureté Longue Mort* . . .

Revenge: on the brink of morning, in full sunlight, a town burst open like a fruit.

Marseilles, end of the line.

The Mac-Loufs, having arrived the day before, were settled in a hotel. The Reverend had retained a none too good impression of his equatorial fold, but would he have better luck here? Let's not be too optimistic. Already, as a sign of a joyous advent, the local papers announced the discovery in the home of the most renowned physician the corpse of a young tax collector who had been missing for months. It had been expected he would be found alive and debauched in some house of ill fame. But instead he had been content to putrefy quite submissively in the house of an easygoing healer who had been metamorphosed into a murderer by his mistress's excessive demands.

A simple enough story, but one capable of disrupting a city opening on the sea—a city where girls smell of shellfish, and where stevedores with skin the color of their hair, after the bath that cleanses them of the sweat of the docks at the close of day, bulge with far prouder chests than those of the whistling laborers of the capital.

Saint Mac-Louf, those fresh-complexioned marionettes promised to lead you a merry dance. And what words could bring back to the straight and narrow path sailors who had slept in the shadow of bellies of every shade, and whose flesh would relinquish only with life itself the perfume of salt and adventure? Marseilles, brown of skin beneath the blood of your body's trunk, you were not putting on an act. The child who was almost a woman accepted with a throb of the heart each of the glances that slipped so gently from under passing lids ... Condemn as the missionary might those minutely stepped dances by which vagrants enthrall the esthetes of the entire world, or denounce as he would the feigned ingenuousness of the too small shoes that cause Roumanian women to marvel, or the carnation behind the ear, or those whirling javas that put red patches of desire on the faces of Anglo-Saxons of every age, sex, and denomination—still the lightest slap of the mechanical piano would continue until the end of the world to arouse seaport nights to howling folly. A conflagration of songs was ignited by the setting sun, and the child who was almost a woman knew she betrayed her world by going to the little rectangular square where sailors of the entire world displayed the bazaars of their desires. Torsos molded of joy, faces carved out of contempt, lips swollen with cruel strength, what could men of bone and black broadcloth do against this tide of flesh? Mac-Louf distributed kilos of pious booklets in neighborhoods that his wife called "bad." Read, rather, this little pink leaflet that escaped from between the pages:

If you desire the forgiveness of God in accepting the Lord Jesus Christ as Saviour and Divine Master, in accordance with the simple word of the Gospel, and apart from all that men have invented and embellished, we will be happy to send you free the New Testament and some booklets, and to enter into correspondence with you.

Write to Mr. Core, c/o Mr. Willy, 310 Boulevard Chape, Marseilles.

The forgiveness of God. A fine disconcerting formula. But what could this hypocrisy do against such widespread insolence?

The pardon of God. They had such good muscles, these fellows, and the girls had such a great liking for those muscles, while Mac-Louf and his gang amused them as would a Punch and Judy show or a parade. In the gentle shadow of *bistrots*, when they had nothing better to do, with one hand shading their eyes, they leafed with the other through these books. Between two parables, they took great pleasure in small but knowledgeable sips of an absinthe-like aperitif, surprised, however, to learn that there were people rotten enough to throw stones at an adulterous wife.

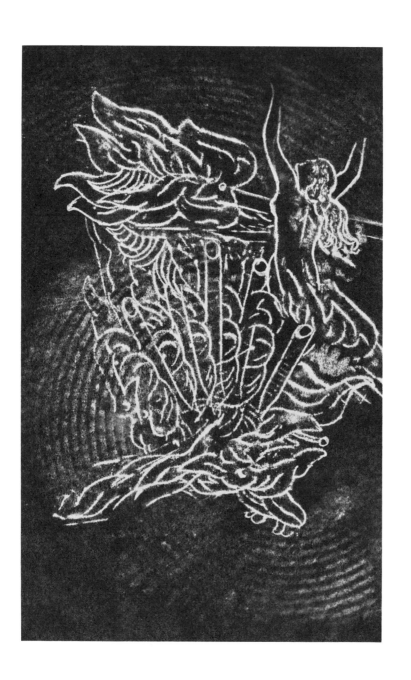

It wasn't long before the little Negro girl, unhampered by fidelity, tried out the amorous resources of this city of flesh. Here she was coming home at dawn deliciously worn out. Her lips kept the memory of kisses that smelled of red wine, of virility well baked by the sun, of garlic and ferocity. On her breast, between her skin and the linen blouse, was pressed the Gospel according to St. John, given her at the moment of farewell by her night's companion, a departing sailor who had received the entire holy collection the day before. In the gentle season of peonies, bodies after lovemaking have the odor of warm bread. The tars who sail tomorrow will, with quivering nostrils, grant today all that is wished for by handsome Englishmen, colonial couples, and ageless little girls. How many times have two legs felt the vibration, well regulated and repeated, of a vigorous mystery? But in thanks for the bank note or the lisping song that paid for their rough caresses, to all those, male or female, who encountered their desire, these shameless and generous kids (who earned five *sous* a day) handed out one of the Reverend's books. In two-line pica and rose, blue, or sandy covers. A little Negress slipped the souvenir booklet under the bolster at night beside a cherished fetish she had secretly kept. In the morning, Mac-Louf asked her if she did not feel happier since leading a Christian life. She answered yes with her eyes, but could not help smiling at the sweet candor of evangelical missions, so cheerful under the melted lead of the most relentless of Africas, or else buffeted without concern on the most treacherous of waters. Their cargo of loincloths, madapolam drawers, calico skirts and scapulars, could not prevent the flowering of desire. In the heavy hours, there was not a glance that was not alight with a new cupidity; and from the dark surge of uniforms the sailors of the entire world made their escape into the rosiest and most nude of Resurrections.

Shoes with light tops, shirts of the same color as those ten-*sou* ices that perfume the innocence of mouths, Amie needed only to set her foot on the quay to feel immediately a sudden hunger spring to life. Everywhere in the city, there were much too handsome, much too edible, gigolos. Her maiden voyage in voluptuousness had famished her even more. As Petitde-mange epitomized for her all this untried flesh, what a fine tumult was their first night in the Hotel Beauvau! Because it was months and months that she had been deprived of a con-fidant, the next day, when her granddaughter came to visit her, the amorous blonde described her many joys. She tossed off names of rivers, mountains, deserts. She hadn't forgotten the name of a single hotel, where deep kisses succeeded in fath-oming the mysteries of the day. The drinker of kerosene (who, let it be said in passing, had just been condemned to life im-prisonment) had once picked the gaudily colored roses from the evil wallpaper of furnished rooms. But Amie, she knew how to arrange the most subtle bouquets in the shade of walls that sheltered the blossoming of her delights. Daughter of Eve, after the long patience of her life, what a revenge! At first, liberty had been for her an empty space. It seemed to her that she had just given birth. She had been relieved of a heavy bur-den. But since for so many years she had grown accustomed to it, no longer to feel herself heavy with a weight of servitude made her believe she would never recover her equilibrium. So it is with the young mother who leaves her bed with her belly abruptly uninhabited. But quickly these slim creatures recover their suppleness, so that it seems barely possible that worry, a threat, or even a simple expectation had once filled their wombs.

Amie, who had swapped her classical repertory for one more worthy of her new existence—and had not asked that Petit-demange's caresses be sanctioned by her offspring—Amie cited Baudelaire:

The glacial majesty of the barren woman.

The glacial majesty of the barren woman. And, indeed, what impassive grandeur as she retraced the phases of her extraordinary destiny. Without holding her tongue for a single instant, she could have continued for a fortnight the account of her adventures. She had seen everything, experienced everything. Not a single hour but had paid tribute to her insatiable curiosity. The last minutes of the homeward voyage were not the most banal, for the crew, thanks to the pretext of the reduced rates of the crossing, had persuaded a number of Africans (for who could teach the children of the sun to fear the heat?) to let themselves be roasted beside a boiler. So when it was a matter of unriveting the sheets of metal that held captive these unusual passengers, instead of brown-skinned men they found men blue, mauve, and beige. With quivering nostrils, Amie, who not only had the colors of wild animals but their pitiless nonchalance as well, got drunk anew on the mere memory of the moldy stench of those African stiffs when the abominable surprise had exploded, for—as a final bouquet—already the mundane soil of France was at a distance of but twenty or thirty yards.

Amie described the rippling waters, glossed with tar, perfumed with orange peel. What a magnificent tomb if only the sailors had had the good sense to wait before liberating their suffocated Berbers. Stones in their pockets instead of the shabby rainbows of Moroccan wallets, for weighted bodies take on sufficient discretion. Then nothing would have been easier than to let them slide gently, gently, into the most secret of liquid obscurity, which later, in a few hours, at dawn, would again become the sea, and life.

But as an escort of honor for the father and Cynthia's ship, which was to dock the following day, might not these Africans, amateurs in bargain trips, have been recovered from the bottom of the sea? Legs of the drowned, worn thin by the invisible caprice of tears, in underwater precipices you found a way to flourish anew in a transparent life of fins. Electric monsters lit up. Question marks with equine heads, sea horses ascended vertically. Algae soared in *Arcs de Triomphe*. A woman welcomed the homage of the waves, but with lifted eyes still followed the phantom vessels inscribing their course on the open sky. Star of Cynthia, the auburn-haired, fixed star of brimstone and love, over there, very far, further, higher than the horizon and than habit, farther than liberty, that inexorable leech upon universal falsehood, star whose spirit can make geysers leap on high, and streets disjoin the pavingstones with which man's hypocrisy had clothed the nourishing soil, whose mirage in the deceptive appearance of a magistrate's blond beard had, in moral rectitude, made off with the spouse of a celebrated psychiatrist, in exchange for the indefatigable temptation of preposterous continents and inclement seas; O, sun, who strikes blows of madness on the frailty of hearts and skulls, you alone can accept the regard of innocence without turning deathly pale when tomorrow a woman with a scarf of wind will cross the canicular! She will be the stranger on the threshold of the streets. Her companion, the father, will have eyes as yellow as if of a metal that will not be gold. The rags hanging in the windows in honor of this couple will applaud in every color, and summer for one day, one single day, never to be forgotten by the creatures who will have lived through it, summer will not tolerate the least penumbral precaution.

Cynthia, drenched by breezes coming from one knows not where, you are the bridge from the minuscule and precise planet to a supreme mystery. You are the one who confuses scruples and scrofula, unable to remember which of these syllables, too clammy to touch, refers to the vacillation of fabricated justice, which to the malady that softens bones, rips open muscles, rots the glands.

Fragile and invulnerable, your disdain for others (all others who are not the silent lover) protects you from the temptations of mundane pride. You *are*, without seeking to know what, how, for whom, why. You see no reason to interest yourself in the fate of your vagabond self, to pity yourself rather than pity a bunch of roses dying of heat in a florist's window, or rather than the florist herself, or for the first pebble struck by the toe of your shoe.

This was why, when you walked between the child becoming a woman and her father in the high flaming noon, everything that could reflect your image revealed you as sister to the walls and the pavingstones where, for days on end, each pinpoint of sun was extinguished, its drop of useless color lost in the mesh of stones. Had you been vain about appearances, then you might have rejoiced, for even the heat proved you as little as possible like other creatures, who puff themselves up, oscillating and giving the impression that if they took a fancy to the sea over there, their bodies would detach themselves from the earth and somehow fly, twins of the Montgolfiers whose zigzags and uncertainties above the trees haunted the nightmares of childhood during the season of carnivals in the cities of health spas.

The hour smelled like a varnished toy, of stable straw, fried food, half-melted ice on the fish that cannot help itself, of sherbets made of stagnate water, of sausage, and gestures void of joy.

Rainbow of irony, under the psychiatrist's panama, under the Reverend Mac-Louf's black straw hat with wide, flat brim, concupiscence touched up the little heaps of bone and hair that served as faces. Neither one nor the other seemed to recognize those they had just passed. Doubtless it was because in the entire universe they could no longer see anything but a girl's two enormous calves. Like an edema, desire stretched their withered skin. And yet Cynthia remained fresh as a cherry amidst all the whirling, reeling rush of those stained with indigo by the lantern of a brothel, others by the lilac mold of the hypocritical silence of a church, still others by the habitual boasting of advertisements' lies. All that breathed was blue, green, purple, violet, yellow. But though the sun pinned top-heavy bouquets in greasy heads of hair, ignited breasts with insolent festoons or struck them with a fiery hand, and laid on the animals themselves all it had taken weeks to wrest from the weary brown of the earth, from the impertinence of shops, the weariness of leaves, there remained a woman whom the madness of the day could not defile.

Cynthia, daughter of Snow and Mirror, your soul was a miracle without gesture, without image, the brook that mirrored itself, where no Narcissus would ever find, to cherish and to lose there, his own pitiful humanity. You went on your way, and over the city the sky, elusive brother of the waves, was hollowed to such depths that of all the lovers in the entire world the father and you alone dared touch it that night in dreams.

Beer-tavern romances grating on the nerves, the enticing pliancy of felt coasters under iced drinks, the leather of benches soothing feverish palms, a marble-topped table, the fact remained that love is still not a simple remedy. Already the girls selling kisses, the hooligans, and the all too compliant sailors no longer heard the serenades or gave a thought to their own chicanery. At the meshing of the crossways, vampires suddenly hesitated, more timid than flies exploring spider webs. And all those of either sex for whom the sidewalk had become a tightrope, ceased their dances. The little jackets of blue linen drooped, pathetic wings no longer brave enough for a new flight. And these bits and pieces of fanfaronade, with caps jerked over one ear, suddenly raised themselves up to bow to the grandmother whores.

Cynthia, Cynthia, behold your miracle.

You were even more beautiful than the child becoming a woman had imagined. She wanted to know your entire history. Not only the story of your love, your travels, but the life you led before you found happiness, before the triumph. And so you talked of your early years, of your English countryside, of a little graveyard scattered in the grasses around a church. Your sad adolescence, thinking unceasingly of death, until the day you entered by chance a grocery store all aglitter with ads, and out of hatred for Bovril and chocolates from Lyon, you resolved that you would live.

One fine morning, an invitation from Amie decided you to leave your rose-colored, orphan home. Farewell to the lawns, to walls overgrown with ivy. You didn't leave much of your heart behind. It was years and years ago, when you were fifteen,

that a boy came along who loved to plunge his fingers into the fire of your hair. He left on a trip, and now he sleeps, turned to marble, under the Southern Cross. Shrewder than a Chinese paintbrush, illness got the better of that black virgin he called his future. Brother to fish, to sea-stars, to coral reefs, a lace of fins blows lightly over his great, immobile dream and the scales are no longer cold on his white belly. At the bottom of the ocean, his head is now the most precious of petrified sponges, and evanescent columns of air bubbles rise from his mouth, his nostrils, to the undulating roof of the waves.

But, Cynthia, would you ever have known any other love if Amie, mouthpiece of destiny, had not summoned you to Paris? From the instant you left, you had already foreseen your marvelous fate.

You remember in London, where you spent several days before sailing for France, a little bar, exotic because of its longing to be Parisian, with rootless vegetation in bowls, black seats, and complicated glass work on its washable walls. There, one evening, in one stroke, the memory of all previous minutes was wiped out. Because you had red hair, you were taken for a Frenchwoman. Your neighbor in the next room had recognized you in the perfume shop where you had just discovered "Rose-Géranium." He spoke to you of the strange house in which you and he lived, praised this place on the summit of which one could sleep and make love, take baths and showers in the middle, and on the ground floor, among the arocarias, the cactus, the dwarf palms, pass entire nights getting drunk in the company of obstinately nocturnal Berliners and Judaique-Saxon esthetes. You dared not tell this man (whose memory would later be called the man without a face) that it was chance alone that had brought you to this place. Silent and

superior, you accepted the parallel between Renoir and Cé-
zanne that he undertook to explain in order to seduce you.
Then he spoke to you of a young genius in Chelsea; of the
fashion for massive ivory bracelets that ossified into Negroid
serpents the arms of a strange young woman; of the bristling
collars of feathers such another wore around her neck. The
man without a face proceeded to advise you to write, and you
didn't even listen to him. Only because you thought he considered it a bit dumb for a young woman of your age to arrive
virgin in a France where you believed sensuality flourished, you
consented to spend the night with him. An indifferent appren-
ticeship. At dawn, he opened a large suitcase, took out some
long bamboo stems, pipe bowls of silver and jade, and lit a little
lamp. And you accepted that your body become transparent.
The next day the man without a face would leave for India. As
souvenir of the service he had rendered you, you accepted a
small amount of his drug, and all that was needed to enjoy it.

Then, what a marvelous noon hour after the long, immobile
morning. You are all alone before your mirror. Your ears are
too pretty to be shown both at once. You shake your head of
hair, and in one fell swoop you toss the entire mass of it to the
right. On the left, a transparent, rosy shell lies on a bed of
flaming seaweed. Then, satisfied, you go toward the house
where there is no other light than the flaming caprice of fish
behind glass.

Balloons of hope, frenzied stars, thickets of hatred, rainbow
bubbles, orchids of love, treacherous morning-glories, rum-
blings of thirst, mollusks of the sea and blossoms of the waves,
diaphanous doves, birds of the water's canopy, what a dawn at
the bottom of the sea has painted these acrobats with mother-
of-pearl! Unknown suns had left such rays upon their tights

that simply to look at them, Cynthia, made you radiant for life. Glide on, you eels, you who came down from the mountains, where you are snakes, to go into the deepest chasm of the Sargasso Sea and knot yourselves one with the other. The mauve fish-mouths of mute singers knock against the panes of glass. The center of a monstrous onyx is alight with a magnificent fire, although in the dust of its exterior facets tiny monkeys of nothing at all compel mockers to cease their laughter and to recognize on those animal faces their proudly human pain. But the cynocephali and their more than satisfied desires were not made to amuse you, strolling lady. And what did their giant brothers matter, those whose only sport was to metamorphose banana peels into delicate flowers?

In the middle of the day, in the largest capital of Europe, you felt your forces gathering strength. The grass was green, the sun round, and the roads that crossed the park of plants and animals were simpler than paths through the fields. You went your way ashamed of one part of the world that must ask others for their wild beasts, beasts who would never again be able to utter those great cries that rend the forest. Try as it would to imitate Africa, this jungle of gaudily painted iron, of central heating, was the sly snarl of exiles instead of the jungle's hoarse, free song. The fetid incense of giant turtles, the absurd anger of lions, the insults of tigers, the disdain of panthers, the coquetry of cobras too sleek to be honest, the deceptive sleep of crocodiles—Cynthia, you were never to forget the cages and the aquariums in the middle of the green lawns, but because neither that exceptionally flat fish, nor that octopus, nor that cheetah, were to fix your destiny, you abandoned this Zoo without looking back.

The same evening, at seven o'clock, you would be in a capital the other side of the Channel, and you would accept an entire family because of an all too handsome son-in-law, whose eyes will seem to you the same color as the sky, the sky of Havana that would not be blue but tobacco. Thanks to the gift of the man without a face, this brown-azure will little by little metamorphose into a yellow metal. Thus he should be doubly praised, he who, having operated on your virginity, made you the additional present of a valise of dreams. You travel with your paradise, and certain hours of each one of your days are oases of immobility.

However, the moment has come to call a halt. You have walked the streets of flesh. For the child becoming a woman, you have spoken. But it is late, mysterious one. You are the passerby. You must say adieu. Tomorrow you will leave again for your native fogs. In a red and gray city, you will have a colorless room with silver walls, its windows open to the clouds, whose sister you are. It is in the wide open sky that one must seek the gestures of your fingers, the shadow of your face.

★
★   ★

Legs spread, a city falls asleep, naked on the phosphorescent sea.

CHAPTER SEVEN

The Indifferent Triumph

This slumber, watched over by Cynthia's luminous shadow, asked only that it might endure until the consummation of the centuries or, failing eternity, at least to be voluntarily prolonged a few more hours into the morning, but Mrs. Mac-Louf precipitated herself headlong into the room, and despite her usual calm, began screaming louder than if the house were on fire.

Then, throwing her daughter down at the foot of the bed, she covered her body with a kimono, and pushed her into the adjoining room where, slumped over a stack of pious pamphlets, the missionary presented in his entire aspect an undeniable perplexity. He scratched his apostolic brow, bit the nails of his consecrated hands, groaned, implored:

"Undoubtedly you could help me, my child. Your assistance is my last hope for salvation. Our young catechumen seemed to have a genuine attachment to you, and you yourself have been exceedingly kind to her. Moreover, haven't I considered her somewhat as if she were my own daughter? So listen: this poor little creature is lost, assassinated, run away, I don't know what. On waking up, your honored mother, surprised that she hadn't come as usual to open our shutters and disturbed by an absence that, in all Christian charity, she at first attributed to some kind of illness, hastily slipped on a dressing gown and went to knock on her door. She called her name. No response. She went in. No one. As the bed was not undone, Mrs. Mac-Louf deduced that the servant had spent the night outside. We summoned the hotel porter. Under persistent questioning, the man finally admitted that he did, in effect, recall having seen the one we were looking for go out, but he had not seen her come in. We notified the police. Seaports, alas, are not lacking in caltrops. Has the poor child been raped, shipped off?"

"Indeed, indeed," observed the psychiatrist, "if it were not in this instance the case of a colored girl, I could almost believe we were in the midst of the white slave traffic. But with a Negress . . ."

"Hey, hey, a Negress, and this one in particular, would be considered a choice morsel! At any rate, a Negress doesn't get lost like a pin. I grant you there are creatures of every skin and color here. But our little savage, whose portrait has appeared in several papers, would scarcely stand the chance of passing unnoticed. And to think that I chose her from among all of them. Among the souls I was guiding, hers seemed the most reliable. I was pleased with her, and her existence—had she continued to live decently and uprightly in a civilized society—would have proved the beneficial influence of our dear League. Let us hope we are not fishing in muddy waters. You will re-

member the poet who evoked: *A Negress shaken by the demon*.
One of my colleagues, who had brought back from a mission
a Senegalese he was proud of, caught the great black fellow
committing reprehensible acts on the person of the custodian
of the temple where he gave his sermon every Sunday. If there
has been a flight, and if my enemies succeed in proving it, I'll
be disgraced and sent to the depths of Patagonia."

"I would follow you there, Reverend."

"You will follow me there, dear wife, and your tender fidelity
will be a great solace. But for the moment, let us act so that
God will not permit his servant to be put to so severe a test.
Besides, your daughter will not fail to help you. I am anxious
to hear her opinion. Speak, my child . . ."

So much the worse for Mac-Louf and the prestige of an
undertaking that would have revitalized with living flesh both
the work itself and the custodian of the chapel. Under questioning, the child did not betray her brown-skinned friend. The
day the little Negress would begin to thirst for the forgiveness
of God, she would be of an age to find quite alone the house
in which she well knew awaited a complete choice of gospels,
holy tracts, sacred pamphlets, and the makings of orations.
Doubtless she was still in no great hurry to return to a diet of
boiled beef and common prayer, for all she truly loved was her
liberty, coconuts, and the thighs of young men, particularly in
the tall grasses of an equatorial noon. (Reverend, Patagonia had
you hanging from her nipples. No better trick could have been
played on you than this departure without fanfare or trumpets.
You were pleased to show off your catechumen, your produc-
tion, as proudly as Vaucanson his automated duck.* And also

---

*Translator's note: Jacques de Vaucanson was a celebrated eighteenth-century me-
chanician, inventor of automated toys.

with what pride you drew photographs from your pocket com-
paring her before and after her conversion, a comparison certainly not unfavorable to you.)

Before. After. As in the shop windows of those who reweave
cloth, there are two squares of identical material, the first torn
down the middle, the second supposed to have been but no
longer torn, so did little Bamboula serve as a sample.

And now, completely black on a mattress hollowed like a
dory by a long night of love, she rubbed herself against him
whom she loved in the manner that she loved. Mattress, beautiful boat, happy voyage, and better luck to the little Negress
than the drinker of kerosene had. Another one flown, and the
cook had been right when she declared: "This family, just like
butter in the frying pan . . ."

Meanwhile, Mac-Louf didn't know which saint to turn to,
which saint or devil to evoke. A bit more and he would have
asked Petitdemange's advice. In this very place, so as to abide
by Amie's will (she who wished never to leave the city of flesh),
the ex-magistrate was continuously on the point of opening an
agency of investigation. All the same, a missionary could
scarcely turn to an aberrant couple. So he pursued alone his
investigations, the center for which was in the brothel quarter,
which, it might be said, he no longer left. Up and down the
streets he went, the length and the width of them. Upon each
of the rooms of pleasure, which opened onto the shops, he cast
an eye. These ladies gave him the nickname Ratichonnet. And
because time dragged as they waited on their doorsteps, they
amused themselves by following Ratichonnet, pulling the tails
of his coat, snatching off his hat, pelting him with stumps of
cabbage. Resigned, he continued on his way, enquiring: "Have
you seen a Negress?" The shrug of shoulders in response had

a rhythm difficult to interpret, the coarse laughter, the loud slaps on all too visible thighs. Moreover, the dirty wenches weren't satisfied with giving Mac-Louf a sobriquet and playing a thousand tricks on him, but they indulged in all too precise familiarities that brought beads of sweat to his brow, made his voice quaver, and caused his thin little legs to give way beneath him.

Reverend, your cross was heavy to bear, and arduous the ascent of that Golgotha that smelled of garlic sausage, of dubious humidity, of counterfeit absinthe and of much-used meat. If you sought to rest, leaning against a wall, a coarse hand covered with zinc rings shook you. The voice of a dark-skinned woman exploded on your weariness like the sun up there on the festoons of rags.

"Hey there, cutie. You're not feeling so good? A little drink? I know some beautiful girls. What about it? Pimp, you don't answer. You must have some kind of vice. Hey, you son of a whore. If it's titillation you need, gorgeous one, we can oblige. I've got some male colleagues, if that's what you prefer. Want one called Lucien? He's been baptized 'The Warbler' here in the quarter because he sings like a tenor. But the cutie's voice isn't the only good thing about him. One night he made thirteen Japs happy. And those little yellow behinds aren't satisfied with promises. If you don't want The Warbler, he has a brother not so young, but even huskier. He's got five women, ladies who work the sidewalks of the Cannebière, plus one of the nobility named Loute d'Oisy, who's on the stage. But are you going to answer, Donkey?"

"Have you seen my Negress . . . ?"

"Your Negress, you give me a pain with your Negress. Ratichonnet, if you want to see her, your Negress, take a look."

A piece of a shift was lifted, and a gesture made with both hands put the man of God to flight.

How was it possible, faced with all these trials, not to regret the time when his existence was already consecrated to vice, only not to the censuring of it, but to satisfying it? Pedlar of dreams, with his cardboard hump, he had wandered across the world. Instead of a Bible, he had bartered the gibbosity of sin. But were not his shoulders still burdened by the guilt that made prostitutes and their friends (the muscular ones and the others, the pretty boys with too rosy cheeks), seeing him come down, harassed, to the city in the evening, smile with an indulgence filled with illusions: "That Ratichonnet, that Ratichonnet . . ."

The Negress, meanwhile, still could not be found. *Coup de Grâce.* One day the grandfather did not come down for breakfast. Was it his turn to run away? They knocked on his door. No answer. They went in and found the unfortunate scientist forevermore immobile on his bed. He had ceased to live. Without a sound, as a fact proceeds from fact to its consequences, from cause to effect, he had passed from life to death. MacLouf rendered homage to this modest death, while his wife sobbed:

"My father, dead in this place, far from his home, in a hotel bed!"

"Your father was called to the bosom of God," corrected the Reverend.

That afternoon, he interrupted his investigations to remain in prayer beside the corpse. Thus the ladies would have the time to busy themselves with their mourning attire. So the missionary began to read the psalms. Suddenly his pious labor was interrupted by the arrival of a blonde woman who was unknown to him, and who began strewing red roses on the pall.

"I am the widow."

"I am the husband of the daughter."
"Your mother-in-law."
"Your son-in-law."
"Your mother."
"Your son."
"You are the husband of my daughter."
"And you the mother of my wife."
"The son-in-law."
"The widow."

A delicate situation. Heaven be thanked that the list of kin continued in declension until the return of Mrs. Mac-Louf.

Then Amie stated with authority:

"Your late father never wanted a divorce. Hence I am his widow. In the presence of death let us forget our mistakes and our disagreements. Let us embrace one another ... I am the one who brought the red roses. He was so fond of them, poor man. You remember your youth, the terrace, the flowers I myself watered with a syringe. My child, faced with the problem of destiny, everything is seen in a new light. Let us be generous. Let us embrace each other again ... One of my friends, Mr. Petitdemange, told me that if he could be useful to you in any way, he was entirely at your disposal. He's very closely connected with the director of the Borniol firm. It is our duty to have a beautiful funeral. Your father was the greatest psychiatrist of modern times. His mushroom-act theory is doubtless debatable. But this doesn't mean it didn't come from a fearless mind. We must honor our scientists. But since your dear husband's vocation makes it necessary for you to travel all over the world, and since I find myself settled down in this city, why not choose it as the final abode of our dear departed one? In this way I could take care of his grave every day, decorate it ..."

"What tact, and what an admirable wealth of charity in that

soul that for an instant went astray!" concluded the missionary after Amie's departure. "Your mother is right, dear spouse, and after all, as she so justly put it, she has never ceased to be your father's wife. His wife before God and man. So, before God and before man, let us forget the past. Besides, for us good was born of evil, and without her guilty love our innocent happiness would not have been possible. Be merciful, then, and with all your soul swear that you have forgiven."

"I have forgiven, Reverend."

★
★ ★

"A beautiful funeral must be as well regulated as a ballet," Amie decided, and she directed with the greatest care the obsequies of the positivist. Nothing was left to chance, to improvisation. Her gown, her linen, her shoes, everything down to the most minute details, had been thoughtfully considered. Upon her arrival at the funeral parlor, she seemed to have become again the woman whom the dead man had called his life companion. She had disguised herself as the woman she once was. The widow's hat let not a single blonde hair be seen. Under veils (which the midday sun made even more black and mournful), she had recovered her virtuous presence, that upstage bearing that led to her being taken for a classical heroine. Lost in the crowd, Petitdemange, judging it more fitting that he not make himself conspicuous, hoped in his heart of hearts that the woman who was soon to bear his name (for now at last it was possible to regularize their situation) would one day follow his own hearse with such dignity, and, finally, with such fidelity.

After Amie came the Mac-Loufs: Madame discreet and re-signed, the Reverend mumbling the speech he would presently deliver at the tomb. The granddaughter of the dead man was the last in the family cortege, followed by a flood of delegations and the merely curious.

The brass of the municipal fanfare reminded the bystanders that death was not such a sad thing. At least not for a choral society. Also, doubtless at least not for a Negress inasmuch as there was the runaway catechumen pressed close to a husky fellow, laughing as hard as she could. But the Reverend, all anxiety over the oration to be given at the tomb, was unaware of this show of contempt. So much the better, for of these two duties, he would certainly not have failed to forget the actual, that of a son-in-law conducting the ceremony of mourning, for the other, that of the shepherd of souls. Then, because of a pair of eyes dancing ludicrously in a face the color of black pearl, he would have abandoned the place that protocol and Amie had assigned him, and in one stroke shattered the harmony of the obsequies. The little savage, who no longer wished to be converted, had, it is true, taken her precautions, and while she was amused by the hearse with its nodding plumes and extravagant wreaths, she called upon the mascot, now restored to its place in her bosom, between the two fresh little breasts, in the very spot where she had had to wear the sacred cross. The idol of her youth, the divinity of fragrant wood, with such a fine, proud physique, a navel of indulgence, thighs of longing, had from beyond the seas watched over her and prevented the triumph of the God of Mac-Louf and of calico-petticoated melancholy. Thus did the daughter of forthright cannibals outwit the cunning of the drinkers of water, and, after making one small gesture to the one who would surely not betray her, she remained cloaked in mystery.

Who, then, could ever get her out of it?

Since the return from the interment, the investigations again began, and were no less in vain.

Petitdemange who, as Amie's future fiancé, had regained an honorable status in the family, was determined to prove that he had lost nothing of the adroitness that had earned him such glory as a magistrate at the time of the drinker of kerosene; but for all of Petitdemange's running hither and yon, and Amie's seeking the fire of her prophetic genius of yesteryear even in the transparence of the faintest sparks of dreams, their activities produced no results.

Mac-Louf, as he expected, received the order to go to Patagonia, where trees are unknown, and the inhabitants are so tiny and defectively proportioned that Mac-Louf himself, according to those who sent him there, would at least have the unexpected happiness in that country of believing himself to be Hercules or the god Mars.

In Patagonia, of all the animals, only the sheep, who are content with so little, find enough grass between the stones to be sufficient sustenance. Hence flora and fauna were meagerly varied. As for the natives, whose legs measure eight to ten centimeters, while their arms in contrast reach to the ground, thus serving as crutches for their precarious gait, they navigate in skiffs of poorly tanned leather that stink of carrion. At night, they bring these clumsy barks back to shore, turn them over, and sleep in their shelter. They wear no clothes, but oil their bodies. From living in the complete solitude of the wilderness, they have, it is said, lost their sense of hearing. In any case, none of them know an articulated language, which was hardly likely to facilitate the mission of the Mac-Loufs. So as to restore their courage, these latter individuals told themselves that Patagonia would have at least one great advantage over Africa, in that it would be much less luxuriant, and not as edible, so that panthers need not be feared; but then they were told that those in charge of the game-bag business were, first of all, the Patagonians themselves, and also that there were perfect jewels of vultures, beautifully feathered, but with claws of steel, which swooped down upon you without warning from a deceptive, icy sky, free of all prejudices, and, lacking a ewe lamb or a native, ready to feast on the male or female morsel of a preaching couple. Thus Madame Mac-Louf, faithful to her promise to follow the Reverend to these desolate territories, left her daughter in France in Amie's tender care.

The embarking: the same brass band played the same airs as for the funeral of the psychiatrist. Enough to give you goose pimples. A movie cameraman. Bouquets, chants, mission banners flapping in the wind. The hawsers were cast off. Amie wept. Petitdemange waved a handkerchief. The ship moved away. Mac-Louf was no more than a black period, his wife a gray comma.

Amie, to change the mood a little, suggested a visit to the villa that was to shelter her happiness, a few kilometers away on a hill amidst salt, sun, and seaside pines.

"We'll have terraces, won't we, dear Alfred? I wouldn't be happy now with a simple belvedere like the one I had on my property in the Seine-et-Oise. We've left a gloomy and boring province for a region of love and fire. So we must have *terrasses*, terraces on which to stroll, to bathe ourselves completely in light and dreams. Terraces and even—why not?—hanging gardens all around the house, and this would be a property that we would call Babylon. Babylon. What do you think of that, dear Alfred?"

"Certainly a fine name. But isn't it a little bit high-sounding, Amie?"

"No doubt, but worthy of our pergolas, our flights of steps, our views, our present joy, our ecstasies to come. I have found a daughter again, a son-in-law, and there they are, sailing perhaps toward death. Am I then a heartless woman, for never in my life have I felt so lyrical, so inspired? If it wasn't for this ridiculous fashion, my widow's weeds and my tight skirt, Alfred, I would dance for you in the sunset. Babylon, Babylon, we are going to live in Babylon . . ."

Babylon.

At the same moment, seized by the same anguish, an ex-magistrate with a blond beard and a young girl began to tremble. There was a fire down there on the sea. The horizon was a taut string of flaming purple, and the sky was stained with blood. A funereal Loïe Fuller, an old woman under her widow's veil, was struck full in the face by great wads of red, blue, and yellow. The hour slapped her with a hand gloved in perfidious azure and flames. She resembled her sister, the owl, when, inscrutable in her billows of crepe, she threatened more tranquil destinies. She saw herself as a creature between two marriages—like a trout between two waters—who, beneath the ceremonial black, allowed just enough as was necessary of her mauve silk underwear to be speculated on; a creature who, at the same time impeccable widow and ardent betrothed, now watched her dream turn to gold in the rays of the city of flesh, and suddenly she alone saw it become a terrifying ballet.

Babylon. Babylon, dance on among the stones that no cement has joined together. Babylon, where are the fingers that will gather together the scattered materials out of which men build their homes? Tonight an unfinished house seems already a ruin, and tomorrow, when taking the promised flowers to the grave of the positivist, Amie will be frightened by Cynthia's face, recognized in the veins of marble. At the time of her honeymoon with the deceased in Switzerland, now almost thirty-five years ago, the young and pure husband and wife amused themselves (an innocent pastime) by seeking in the hodgepodge of rocks, ice, and fir trees of each mountain the features of their parents and friends. But Cynthia, present again through the complicity of a white vein in red stone, Cynthia, why did she haunt the final sleep of a great and honorable man who had cursed her and died without pardoning her for having made a Babylon of his home?

Babylon, always Babylon. On the phosphorescent bed of the tide, the city of flesh spread wide its legs, while its head of glossy hair lay on a pillow of hanging gardens. Its limbs, heavy with clusters of caresses, were the trees, immodest gestures their leaves. Beyond, as guide for the uncertainty of navigators, there was no other lighthouse than a gigantic Phallus. Obscene plants grew everywhere. Petitdemange, however, was shrinking, and his hair was losing its color. The night frightened him. He was no longer up to his usual form. Famished, insatiable, Amie cast about. A butcher boy looked at her and she wanted to suck the blood of animals from his big paws. A young poultry salesman, with his sleeves rolled up, and you too who sold fish and had scales on your fingertips, your thick wrists made promises. Your carnivorous jaws would close on any meat, biting any epidermis with pleasure. So too bad if old age happened to come along.

Amie was no longer afraid of the furrowing wrinkles, and forgot to go to the hairdresser for her weekly henna dye. What did it matter? The universe had found its rhythm again: desire. What good was the metronome of coquetry? Throw your makeup into the sea, women, for the sun has put arrows into the veins of man. Let the flowers of flesh spring to life. The heart could not cease being faithful to Petitdemange, and at the same time not take a stroll in the garden of sensuality. What encounters. The hours there were paved with such concupiscence that each minute was a question of whom to choose for its caprice. The hoodlums of the city of flesh did not make eyes, but mouths. In three twists of their thick lips they ran the gamut of all labial, and other, possibilities, and then whistled. Amie would turn around. Too late. The fresh-complexioned marionette would have already found a taker. One lost, ten found, one needed only to choose among these sailors who produced from their seafaring pants splendid handkerchiefs freshly stained with love and perfumed with tobacco and cognac. Each one of these loafers of the old port, with an oblique glance, and for fifty francs, would promise a skilled and robust virility, a ruddy chest, a hard belly, and thighs that, having dispensed with the hypocrisy of underpants, had the good smell of coarse-grained cloth. And on top of all that, a selection of Missionary Mac-Louf's pious thoughts. By the way, Reverend, since you have again popped up, why not bring back from Patagonia one of those autochthons with legs eight to ten centimeters long, which would certainly be a fine surprise for your mother-in-law who thirsts to know everything?

To know everything. And not only the pleasures of sex.

In a little bar, at the threshold of the rippling, silky water in

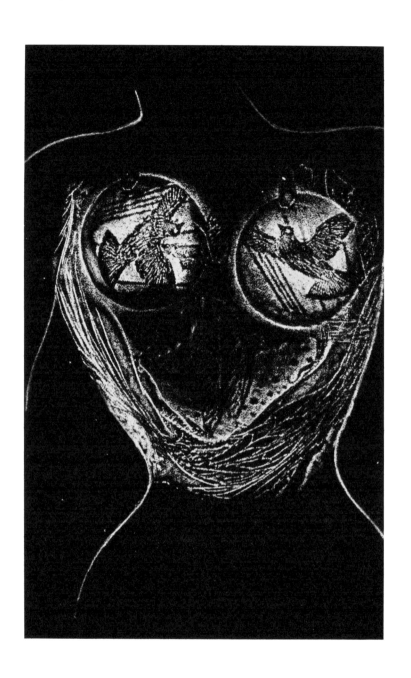

which she liked to think secrets teemed, Amie made the acquaintance of another of Eve's daughters, nicknamed the
Queen because around 1895 she had been the mistress of a
Balkan kinglet. These ladies became intimate very quickly.
The Queen was a jovial toper, and Amie, not wishing to be
outdone, increased her natural high spirits with skillfully mixed
drinks. She would come home, her face aglow, hat awry, speech
voluble but not very steady. Petitdemange no longer dared risk
an observation, and the child becoming a woman felt she had
no right, even in thought, to bring weight to bear on an old
woman who also wanted to revive the wind. Just the same,
Amie could have gone about it a bit better, as Cynthia, in other
days, had chosen the man without a face and accepted the valise
of dreams. But Amie was in awe of the Queen, whose face was
painted with such disorderly violence that it seemed to be made
of pieces picked up here and there at random and put together
any old way.

"Here are our witches," announced the cook whom they had
brought down from Paris, and who was titillated by the Midi.
"What boozy creatures they are! Another Cynthia-like business. A real devil, that redhead. Everyone wanted to copy her,
so it's loonies and company. The young lady of the house is still
the happiest, down there where the savages are, with her one-
yard-square husband. But the old woman with her tricolored
hair—to think I knew that creature, pursed lips, and so proud
that as a joke we called her Madame High-and-Mighty. She's
a case, Madame High-and-Mighty. But she, she's nothing compared to her girlfriend! Did you ever see such a freak, and so
slovenly . . ."

The Queen did, in fact, wear awkward, frayed silk dresses,
made over for better or worse in the fashion of the day. She had

kept the long hair that her royal lover had called the court mantle of his dear favorite. In 1898, when a revolution had forced her to flee, disguised as a peasant, she had taken with her in a potato sack her superb collection of feathers, still intact today, although a little bedraggled.

"I had egrets, puffs, plumes, Amie. You see this amazone? It comes from a felt hunting hat very much in the Mademoiselle de Montpensier style.* I have enough to trim my hats until the end of my days, for you see, from having lived a court life I've kept a taste for decorum. These ridiculous little turned-up hats that are worn now have doubtless a certain cachet. But not two sous' worth of majesty. I love gowns with trains, fantasy, throne-room functions. The King would certainly have married me if his wife—a Hohenzollern, I give you my word—had not held on to him by her miscarriages. Just the same, he would have rejected her. But, alas, he wasn't given the time. He was assassinated. That finished my heaven on earth. Fortunately, I was able to find some small consolation. Ether, morphine, chloroform, cocaine . . . Would you like some? A little pinch?"

"Willingly," responded Amie, not wishing to appear old-fashioned.

★
★ ★

Several days later, Amie confided to the Queen:

"I threw out that Water of Melissa made by the barefoot Carmelites that I've used for my migraine headaches ever since I was of marriageable age. Your white powder, my dear, does

---

*Translator's note: The reference is to Louise d'Orléans (1627–1693), known as the Grande Mademoiselle.

give one fresh courage. The success of my niece Cynthia can now be explained . . . Just another little sniff . . ."

One fine day, the Queen arrived in a state. She was afraid of a police raid. Where to hide her ammunition? Amie had a stroke of genius. In the cemetery, on the tomb of the psychiatrist, there was an urn, the bottom of which no police official would ever think of searching. Each day, under the pretext of prayer, they would go there to reinvigorate themselves.

Babylon, so had the positivist lamented all his life. Babylon, always Babylon, and again Babylon. Amie smiled at the thought of the author of mushroom-acts, the sworn enemy of drug fiends, in his last resting place . . . Even so, for a dead man, he wasn't too much to be pitied. The Widow and the Queen visited him each day. They brought flowers, arranged them, turned this way and that, and the caretaker of the cemetery, seeing them return, sniffling, believed in their tears and pointed them out as an example of fidelity.

From the dormitory of the dead, they would go down to a *bistrot*, or else to a house of worship, for as the Queen, who was at heart a mystic, explained:

"Amie, when I'm fed up, I have only to hear a *Tantum ergo* or a *Kyrie eleison* to get a high. Tomorrow there's High Mass at the cathedral. Shall we go? We'll get behind a pillar . . ."

The High Mass. The organ, the male voices. The Queen, head crowned with a garden of feathers, throat and neck covered by the foam of a boa, sobbed aloud. On the altar was a golden man. Golden as Alfred's beard in days gone by, golden as newly baked bread. Amie wanted to sink her teeth into the beautiful hands at the extremity of the golden man's arms, which he moved in harmonious benedictions. A bell tinkled three times and all heads were bowed. Thus no one perceived the woman who advanced straight between the rows of chairs, and whose ascension, moreover, no one could have prevented, for the power that guided her was already not of this earth. She stretched forth her arms. Another three steps and she could have touched the golden man who smiled at the angels, with no idea of the nature of the fire that lit the face of the approaching woman. But so that he might at last know, so that he understand, a cry, a true cry of the flesh, rent the silence of the church. Amie had leapt upon the golden man, clasped him to her, bit his neck, and this holy priest, who had been faithful to his vows of celibacy and never known love, abandoned his body to the madness of ten agèd ravishing fingers, while a voice howled: "White meat, beautiful white meat!"

★
★ ★

It was said that Amie had gone mad.

Every Sunday, Petitdemange, inconsolable, went to see her. She asked him news of Babylon. When would the palace of their love be finished? In the main *salon*, she wanted a golden throne, with several seats because she wasn't an egoist. The Queen and she would sit there, with dear Alfred between the two of them. But aside from Babylon, how fared the world, the rest of the world? Her granddaughter must be a woman now. "Tell me, Alfred, answer. Is she a woman?"

A woman, yes, a woman, Amie, your granddaughter is a woman, the woman dressed in unbleached linen and crowned with natural straw. The city itself no longer tempts her, and yet, because she does not authorize her indifference to permit her to succumb to the mirages of sleep, of rest, to these oases, she goes on as if, once the threshold of lassitude was crossed, she would have justified her desperate resolution not to be halted even by fatigue.

Disdainful of a choice, of a resting place, she will not ask herself to what or to whom this much-traveled road will finally take her, a road from which the most disinterested of everyday human beings likes at least to derive the notion of a consoling eternity. But because no hopes, no obsessions, such as are common to the masses, because now nothing has the power to assess her, her feet scorn the meanderings of moral expediency and give complete obedience to those invisible gulf streams that, when followed, become subterranean mysteries.

Hence the security of her empty hands, the freedom of her legs, which strive for no fixed end. No need to justify herself weighs on her. An armor of disdain protects her from time and space, and no more than she hears the monotonous song of the streets does she hear the cries of the hours, those great wild beasts that her sidewalk neighbors, men, continue, but in vain, to try to tame. In the place of clocks on the walls, or watches in jewelers' windows, on the thresholds of bazaars, she sees incomprehensible holes. Counting is not her business. Anymore than the city is a sundial. She is the one whom hunger does not hollow, nor anger cause to bristle, whom ennui does not undo. Invulnerable, without there ever having been any need to take her by the heels and immerse her in a river, her fragility, far less precarious than Achilles' power, offers no target to the arrows of the passing moments, to the assault of objects, or to the slyness of individuals. Thus men draw away, shamed by a desire that cannot be fulfilled, inflated with their own importance, but stammering; while women, without overlooking any of their own embarrassment, never dream of degrading with a show of jealousy, the young passerby.

★
★ ★

O strolling wanderer, you who dare look straight into the sky, you, for whom the noonday flames are gentler than the tongues of lions on Blandine's* hands; you, who do not slacken your pace either for the tempting coolness of doorways, or for the acidulated shade of shops where ice cream is sold, or for the illusionary help of tears, while those of the motley crowd bow their heads and reproach themselves because they cannot find again the crown your feet has traced upon the ground.

Like the negative of the will-o'-the wisp's fire, you flutter on, among the ferocities of a circus of dog days indifferent in the blaze of summer, to the hot coals of thirst, to the smoke of hunger. Crowned in natural straw, your head rests as lightly on your body as your body itself, clad in unbleached linen, rests on your ankles. Everything in your person is revealed to be of equal weight. As a triumph in pantheistic unity, your big toe is worth no more nor less than your calf, your brain, or your nose. You are the first not to look on your cranium as a box full of precious thoughts, the first to let your heart beat without considering it a metronome for exceptional feelings.

Now and then you encounter the Queen, and you smile at this poor old piece of decayed meat, which in other days was voluptuous flesh in which each caress had ploughed its furrow, each kiss made its ravine. But when she sees your gentle glance,

*Translator's note: The martyred Saint Blandine was fed to the lions in Lyon in the year 177.

the day becomes a holiday. Her eyes, islands of despair in a crumpled ocean of eyelids, then light up with the sunlight of surprise. She throws kisses to your feet, frailer than birds in their cage of shoes. And, like her, the old streetwalkers, all those who persist in retracing the highway of love, under the rags that clothe them in the shade of the fishbones of their hair, suddenly, and without regret, remember the silks and the long riding skirts of the heyday of their lives.

In their dresses made even out of old curtains, they managed to recreate what in their time was called a bustle, and one could have sworn that these fugitives from the century before last had taken lessons from the celebrated Madame Campan.* On this morning, as on every other, they had made up their faces with beef blood, soot, and Ripolin.† Ever since dawn, they had looked for freshly painted shops so as to steal as much as possible of the rainbow for the faces they cherished even in the most terrifying depths of misery.

Thus, the illusion, this need that impelled the centuries-old wandering Jewesses of love to collect zinc brooches, to make rings out of the tinfoil from chocolate bars, to contrive wigs out of string and wood shavings, to wear tinkling crosses and old corks and pin rotted flowers from garbage cans on the potato sacking of their dresses, this was the dream of grandeur beneath the costumes they wore. The woman crowned with natural straw, dressed in unbleached linen, knew that she was better than these sordid majesties (who could not find even two-*sous* clients yet who wanted to appear higher in rank than their sedentary sisters), as the Queen of the Sabbath Witches

---

*Translator's note: Madame Campan (1752–1822) was Marie-Antoinette's secretary and the author of *Mémoires*.

†Translator's note: Ripolin is the trade name of a well-known decorator's paint.

would be in comparison with a lady president of the Third Republic.

Incredibly wretched souls, corsetted in worldly indifference, justice will finally be rendered you, and your rags will become transparent, so that your wombs will shine through them more luminous than August glowworms, those insects whose bellies are balloons of fire in the tangle of leaves, do you hear, balloons of fire capable of causing moths to die of jealousy on canicular nights.

Bodies heavy with all the lead of human fatigue, without you yourselves knowing how, cling to the subtlest traceries of fog in northern capitals, to the scallops of sun, to the laces of shadow in Mediterranean ports, so that, no longer clutching like the drowning to worldly goals, you become twins of the stars. And your feet will invent a confidence that scorns all pretext, for they will know they were not made for leather prisons, for the torture of pavements, but for the nudity of skin on the nudity of sand.

The dubious hour, then, no longer dared attempt its seductions. Between cast-iron eyelids, the gaslight recovered the original purity of flame, and the heels on which, for centuries, the pleasures of the flesh had floundered, these heels broke suddenly into pieces, while from the macadam sprang flowers no hand had sown. And no lie was any longer tolerated, even were it as slight as soles fashioned of rope. Beyond the horizon, hoodlums tossed away their espadrilles, and the whores were gentle, smoothing their lips with a finger stained with the blood of their last loves. In a plain-dealing city, women no longer took the trouble even to make signs, but turned and turned. The contours of what mystery did they follow, these lady ambassadors of the planets, the stars? Their circular procession hollowed an emptiness around them, and those the quickest to mock drew away, no longer daring to laugh at the unbelievable furbelows these dowagers wore. They alone knew what course to steer on the imponderable pavements. The earth they grazed became lighter than ether, and so badly supported the passerby who watched them that he asked himself how the clouds managed not to fall from the sky; if he followed these vagabonds, it would wreck him, for he had none of the mysterious audacity and scorn that permits the attainment (to a gratuitous degree) of that luminous freedom peripatetics come close to only after myriads of gallant tests, such as the selling of kisses, tears, crimes, and diseases contracted during acts devoid of joy.

But now a woman who had never sullied herself with the purple of curtains from Andrianople, and was too proud to waste time on words or colors, today disrupted the city. A woman more incomprehensible than a diamond whose fire no longer implies gigantic forests in flames, an ocean blazing across the mane of trees, or the work throughout the centuries of subterranean powers.

Woman-child, you will go to the very limits of shade and sun. There, on the threshold of a paradise of tremors and rags, you will stop, a simple figure belonging neither to heaven nor to earth but serving nonetheless as hinge to one and to the other, a frail speck in the great gaping hole of light. You are negative and incorporeal, your only goal being to see and judge without you yourself being seen or judged. Already, girls standing brazenly on the doorstep of their rooms are ashamed of their own lubricity and of their faces that are all painted mouths.

Since a short time there had reigned over this brawling kingdom and these ladies with their bizarre medley of naked flesh, cosmetics, ribbons, and cotton cloth, a Negress who wore violet slippers and a bayadere skirt. If, by chance, someone passed her way without seeming to be concerned with the abrupt laughter of the sovereign or the well-rounded promises in the dressing gowns of her vassals, Her Majesty made a circle of each eye and, at a fixed signal, her subjects and she herself would pick up large quantities of potato peelings, fruit stones, remains of vegetables, refuse, and ordure, which their fingers would mold without prejudice into projectiles to be fired pitilessly at the back of the indifferent passerby. The victim would turn around, and the Negress, more regal than ever, would meet his stare, turn up her lips in a dazzling smile, take hold of her petticoat in both hands, and, after a deep, court curtsy, would in person apologize for this unforeseen mishap in a quarter that, however, had never for a single minute failed to be famed for its reputation of cordial hospitality.

Thanks to speech more humming and lighter than that of noonday bees, words came forth from their everyday cocoons. And behold the sentences of a Senegalese whore winging around a tourist of excessive chastity.

A singular rainbow of multicolored butterflies left the illusion of their pollen on eyes and lips. The tongues that were envious of the rosy-hemmed cavern of the hive at the time of the swarming of syllables had no other temptation than that of a scarlet serpent in a hole of wreckage and shade. And he, in his turn, would succumb, he for whom the mysterious song of the chasms had been resuscitated, chasms in which so many honorable captains had lost body and soul.

Mouth to mouth, lips to lips, at the center of the earth is a kiss. Gulfs of petals are pinned between volcanoes, breasts of a chest with lungs on fire, and the stems of the fluctuating bouquet of oceans do not forget that other flowers of lava and secrecy are unfolding in the depths. To avenge lukewarm hands, minutes without danger but without hope, the heat at the center casts its reflection on that crust where the march of sad insects obstinately takes place. Break the spiderlike legs of the shuddering days, and burst forth, you balloon of leaves that the branches have held in green bondage. Brothers and sisters of the universal kiss have spouted forth living creatures. Listen to their songs, observe their gestures. They are as beautiful as the Cynthia of childhood, more supple than wild beasts, and their skin has the same freshness as that of the legendary shadow, where, once having slept in it, one never wishes to awake. Lift yourselves up, you flaming red curtains. How many days would the ebony Calypso in the farthest depths of her grotto have known how to detain a Ulysses in Oxford trousers? On a shabby sofa, the entire universe was annulled by two feet in violet silk, two long cinnamon-colored legs, and a little rubber mouth lined with coral. The male had no other wish than to pluck all the figs from that one tree.

"Little flower of shoe polish, slithering adder, eel, drop of molten lead, ember of heaven," what names he gave her! The hands pressed on her flanks became heavier than the drunken vessels of death. It would be too simple, travelers, if once and for all the onyx waves accepted to engulf you. One must leave, go on with one's life, and with each step taken in the sun, better and better learn to know that there is no sweeter oasis than the street of the Negress.

In comparison with the sky, all is dust, and yet those booths of caresses were carpeted with a velvet humidity that remained eternally fresh. O day without a soul, there is only one road, that of the flesh, a road one travels thinking only of bodies against bodies, of rafts of nakedness there for other naked-nesses.

Babylon, Babylon, Babylon.

They said you were mad, Amie, and they locked you up. Yet you alone were right. Flesh, beautiful white flesh. Tonight the storm will tear ravenously at the clouds as teeth tear at bellies. In the cemetery, the Queen has consumed in one fell swoop her supply of drugs, and collapses on the cold marble. Babylon, Babylon, Babylon, Amie howls aloud her passion. She is placed in a straitjacket. Babylon. Babylon. Babylon. And that house facing the sea will never be finished. Petitdemange, alone with his blond beard, looks on all this drama as devilishly Ibsen-esque. Happy are those who can escape the debacle in their Patagonia of frozen stones. At least the hearts of the Mac-Loufs are at peace.

For their daily flights in ecstasy, Cynthia and her lover open the valise of the man without a face. Lying on their backs, eyes lost in a delicate sky, they follow ethereal processions, although here the noon hour falls heavier than an iron slab. The sun stabs the city, showing pity only to the street of the whores. Buoyed by desire, these ladies float on a lake of shade while yonder their honest sisters dissolve in the heat. The dog days. Long live the dog days! Are they not called bitches? Then long live the bitch days, the season of spread thighs and heavy teats. And you, famished hordes of males, throw away your socks, your starched collars, your underpants, and your meager brains, and give the last spark of your poor marrow to this display of meat. But watch out. Today the blood is near the skin. But all the same, that's no reason to be afraid: what, it's enough to keep you from daring to go closer? And those suddenly motionless women? A piercing shriek. The Negress has fallen over backwards. Fallen stark dead, because all of a sudden she had recognized the woman crowned in natural straw, dressed in unbleached linen, and all of a sudden she could not take any more. A white funeral will be given you, dear savage, convert of the pious Mac-Louf, but the other one, that quasi-transparent creature who has heard at the threshold of your paradise the one syllable in which the final moment of a life summed up the world's whole amorous agony, how could she not have guessed that you were the little black sister of Cynthia, and of the drinker of kerosene, of Amie, of the Queen, of the wandering Jewesses of love, and of herself . . . ?

Lighter than a shadow, she took flight.

She had not had the luck to encounter, as you did in another time, Cynthia, the man without a face. A lad who resembled at the same time the one of Agrippa d'Aubigné Street and the father, with skin the color of his hair and eyes the color of Havana's sky, he alone had looked gently on her.

He had the pride of those who load and unload ships, his muscles outlined under the coat of tan the sun had woven on his skin.

Except for the azure canvas of his slacks, he was naked. Naked as joy, as rivers, as stones. Naked like the grass, the gums, the teeth. He smiled. But the woman did not respond to his smile. Get along with you, you handsome scamp. You were at the edge of the waves. You began to dance on their crests. Someone over there, very far away, had stitched the sky to the sea. Buffoon of the tides, forget a street that smelled of a cellar and of violet-scented face powder.

Boy, you were much too fond of the festoons of your steps. A woman was there and you merely glanced at her fragility.

Noon. At that particular hour, at that particular age, Cynthia was looking at the acrobats of mother-of-pearl and the opal balloons in the firmament of the sea. You celebrated the anniversary at the threshold of a paradise of shivering and rags, but no more than Cynthia in her aquarium did you turn again toward your sisters with their legs spread apart. Silence. Memory was no longer a gentle poppy. Go down to the harbor, walk forever scornful of time and space. Finish the purple morning among bouquets of shells. Continue walking, and not a word of despair. A dubious rainbow follows the rippling whimsy of the tides. You remembered the drowned men Amie liked to imagine in this tossing grave. You, you saw yourself as Ophelia gliding on the oil that stains the sea. And with what would you replace those long purple flowers the young girl wreathed around her brow before going to the brook, those long purple flowers that virgins call dead men's fingers but that silent shepherds describe by a less circumspect name? You saw yourself, your hair sticky from the violet shellfish that fishwives sell with a little wink of the eye to travelers who wonder for what stupefactive these obscene fruits of the sea were torn from the rocks.

Woman crowned in natural straw, the blue of tenderness must be renounced, the red of desire, the yellow of joy, and even the mauve of fatigue. On the quays, casks slowly lose their perfume interwoven with geranium. Insensitive earth, empty hour, Babylon, after the cries, the scars of teeth, there is a great silence. A jetty draws out to sea this carnal soil, this great body of a continent that sunstroke has beatified.

A woman, a city, compete in indifference.

Afterword:

A Conversation with René Crevel

There were three of us in the Coupole Bar with René Crevel that October afternoon—Anna Balakian, David Rattray and I, who am now setting down at least a partial record of the words and the ideas that we exchanged. Because it was still early there were no other customers in the long, narrow thoroughfare of the bar that by evening would be feverishly alive with the traffic of uneasy women and men. And we ourselves were not entirely at ease as we sat at the table farthest from the rest of Montparnasse with glasses of white wine or Pernod or Vichy Célestin before us. Anna Balakian sat beside me on the leather of the *banquette* that ran the length of the wall under the massively framed mirrors, René and David opposite us on chairs with spindly, iron legs, chairs I seemed to have known all my life. This was a meeting of farewell, an occasion we tried to fill with talk other than that of departure, because René was unexpectedly going away.

That evening he would be on his way to Switzerland, to a sanatorium in Davos, where he had been before. His doctor had advised this in the hope that a time away from the tyranny of the city, two or perhaps even three months of breathing high mountain air, of eating meals at regular hours, of "relaxing," the doctor had said (as if René knew the meaning of that word), would improve his health. A few years earlier, René had written from Davos to a friend:

> *Here always the same life . . . I have too much time ahead of me and not enough hope. In taking care of oneself, one becomes an egoist, an egoism of the dullest kind. And youth so quickly spent, so badly spent.*

And in that letter he also wrote: "I have a novel, *Babylon*, that will come out in October, as well as my lecture, published by the Cahiers du Sud."*

René never wasted time in speaking of his health, and he did not have the mien of an ill man. (Marcel Jouhandeau has written of his unchanging, adolescent beauty, of his ash-blond hair, and the light that always shone so joyously in his eyes, a light that no offense, no betrayal, no discourtesy could dim.) His deepest concern was not for himself, but for the society against which he protested, and for the clearing of the way (as he described it) for the young European to sing the songs of his anxieties. At one moment during the conversation at the Coupole, he spoke of love, poor, overworked love, perhaps because he cherished friends with such tenderness and ferocity.

L'Esprit contre la raison (Marseille: Cahiers du Sud, 1927).

There, on the other side of the table, he was to all appearances a young man in possession of great wealth of every kind: the wealth of a contemplative aristocracy of the mind, endless funds of both material and spiritual solvency, and the incalculable fortune of good health.

"Love has got beyond any claim to good or bad," he was saying to us. "Rather, quite simply, love makes everything bad into something good, and from a minus makes a plus."

And here David spoke of René's third novel, *La Mort difficile* (*Difficult Death*), which he was then translating.

"That transformation from a minus to a plus is the whole gist of *Difficult Death*," he said, "although some American publishers I've sent excerpts of it to don't see it that way. To them, it's 'negative' because of the suicide. But you're not writing exclusively about sexual love."

"It scarcely matters whether the sex in it is good, bad, or nonexistent," René said quickly, almost impatiently, as he had perhaps written or said it a hundred times before. "The joy that comes from it makes anyone who has experienced it feel discontented with so little. . . . But I must admit the physical act that sets it all in motion has never revealed to me anything of essential value."

"Are you saying there are other ways?" David asked.

"A common faith, for instance," René said, alive with eagerness to make us understand. "A common faith provides the possibility of cherishing another person more than one's self, and does it so much better than a mutual need for orgasm. As possibilities go, that's a joyous one. A common faith, a communion of souls, a Jewish vagabond's dream. It overthrew all the so-called wisdom of the ancients, defeated the very laws that did him in. Salvation isn't in some chosen creature or some earthly effort, but it is total and absolute fusion. Lautréamont says everybody is going to be a poet."

"And Breton says," said David, "that the act of love and the act of poetry are incompatible with reading a newspaper out loud."

"But there won't be any newspapers!" René cried out. "It will be a whole new race of people! Lovers, poets, one and all! I spoke of this in *Diderot's Harpsichord*," he went on with it, trying anxiously, fervently, to make it clear. "There I used the term 'sentient harpsichord' for a person who trains his mind to close the gap between his own waking dream and reality. In the 1700s, someone imagined a color harpsichord. I imagined another harpsichord, one with thoughts and feelings like a person. . . . A poet is a sentient harpsichord, alive to the slightest touch, and this makes it a tricky instrument to play. It takes a special kind of diligence."

"The diligence of lightning," David said, and he mentioned a Japanese print he had seen once, and that he could not forget, a delicately executed print of a flash of lightning in a waterfall.

For a moment, Anna and I did not understand this metaphor, and then we saw the pain of René's leaving, helplessly and without warning, present in David's eyes. René had turned his head away so as not to see the reflection of it, and he said (in what may have been gentle rebuke):

"Poetry that delivers us from the symbol sows liberty itself."

"You shied away from verse so as to filter prose with all the freedom of the poet, René," Anna said. "Doesn't your work tell us that poetry isn't emblem, it isn't contrived rime or rhythm schemes, but the symptom and substance of a liberated mind?"

And as if Anna had broken a spell, the grieving of violins,

of many violins playing on a far stage, in a distant concert hall, no longer pled for time, just a little more time, before the curtain would descend. The violins now swept of their own accord into cavatinas and scherzos and ariettas, into waltzes of swirling triumph such as René loved dancing to, turning at last in tender relief to Wolfgang Mozart's ribaldry.

"But isn't it a truly magnificent and almost unhoped-for victory to have this new liberty, this leaping of the imagination in triumph over Reality, smashing the bars of Reason's cage and—bird that it is—obeying the voice of the wind, and detaching itself from the earth to soar higher and farther?" René asked us in delight. "The responsibility, wonderful responsibility of poets! With a single thrust of the fist they've pushed back the horizon, and there in the middle of space discovered an island, the island that we touch with a finger."

"I like your way of expressing man's obsessive dream of levitation," Anna said, "of going beyond what we know, but in a reality that's within the reach of one extended finger."

"Or of one toe feeling its way to the ultimate rock," René said, and perhaps it was the picture of it in his mind that made him laugh.

"We're pushing around such a heavy cargo of liberty, love, and poetry," Anna said (and because René laughed, we three laughed too), "that perhaps we're guilty of that 'psychodialectic' activity you deplore in Freud."

I had just finished the translation of *Babylon*, working not from the published book, but from René's typescript, as he had asked me to. I had with me in the Coupole Bar that afternoon a carbon of my two hundred or so typed pages, and he would take it with him to Switzerland, to read it in peace and quiet there. And he would take with him as well the words of an

Italian poet, words that he had never heard spoken, nor read in a letter, nor seen printed on a page, but words so like his own that it was at times difficult to know which of the two poets was calling out to the other across the brief interval of years. The Italian poet, Emanuel Carnevali, had written of Rimbaud that "anyone who has not dropped his useless burden and gone on a great adventure can understand him. . . . Rimbaud is the Advent of Youth. Almost everything else in the world is unbelief in youth: diplomats, statesmen, chiefs of all works, generals. . . . Almost everything else in the world except for the poets, who have all believed in Youth, is a consecration of the error that life is from youth up; it is from youth down."

And René, the French poet, wrote that the poet by his very nature does not lull his wild beasts to sleep so as to enable him to play the role of trainer, "but, cages wide open, the keys thrown to the wind, off he goes, a voyager who does not think of himself but of the voyage, of beaches of dreams, forests of hands, animals of the soul, of all undeniable sur-reality." For him, Rimbaud as seer, as medium, was "the first to find the *salon* at the bottom of the lake," a *salon* that spread out, hollowed the earth beneath it, multiplied itself "until it became a city in which its secret was no longer a mask," and revealed its true features: love and poetry.

Carnevali's words hastened on, for, nearly a decade before the book was written, he was quite unknowingly declaiming his own introduction to *Babylon*. "To have myself in the days of my youth," he was saying, "with every inch of my body tense, looking, and listening, and interpreting, the dualism of body and soul and the dualism of life and immortality being then risible questions, the appropriate doubts of people who have lost both things, both times, forever. . . . To mould myself then through a long, immense and reasoned upheaval of the senses. . . . In Rimbaud the old words woke from their death-sleep and sang again with the power that was theirs before cowards drugged them." In this he is speaking of René Crevel's anomalous language, so foreign to many, which gives power and grace to the tragicomedy of *Babylon*. "Rimbaud said gloriously that the attainment of poetry is the attainment of life," Carnevali said at the end, "and critics are dead leaves lying still while the hurricane sweeps by, high above."

It was perhaps then that David Rattray ordered another round of drinks, and began speaking to René about "the sin of pride," a sin that Max Ernst, he said, claimed was actually a virtue.

"The virtue of pride in past eras is seen by Ernst as having been a part of the value and beauty of human beings," David said, "at least until it was wiped out by Christian humility."

"The only pride I have ever experienced," René said, holding nothing back, "was on those days and nights I felt myself to be an anonymous parcel of a universal continent whose frontiers were the randy eyes, ears, and nipples, the fears, the wishes, the thirsts, the desires, the rages, the hopes, and the despair of all people. At such times, I let go, and abandoned any effort to pin myself down to a notion of individual happiness."

"But wait a minute," Anna Balakian interrupted him. "You're dealing in abstractions, and that's confusing. I know it's natural to associate Hegel with abstractions, for he was a philosopher. But he said that knowledge is the eternal and infinite rapprochement of thought with its object. He expressed great admiration for metaphoric language. In fact, he called it the supreme activity of the mind."

"The writer has to make his own metaphor," René said, "and

that metaphor unmasks and exposes its author." And he might have been saying that the universal continent was the metaphor he had chosen. "But there's a degree of personal responsibility involved as well," he went on, "inasmuch as the randy eyes, ears, nipples, fears, wishes, thirsts, desires, rages, and despairs of a certain René Crevel, who went out cruising in the rain and was aroused by certain encounters on more than one street corner, loved or hated without even getting his own thoughts sorted out, no matter what the price in misery. They were, these encounters, like the lights that illuminate the hull of a ship on a voyage outside Time and Space, like the antennae of an ideal place that there is no other name for than Paradise, Paradise Regained."

"You are saying that in *Difficult Death*," David said, "when you describe the experience of total love being like a glove turned inside out."

"The Mind turned outward for a change," René said, "and Reason folded under. A long time ago I wrote something about Reason creating so many mindless divisions, such as mind/body, spirit/flesh, real/unreal, sane/insane, dream/action, that Mind was obliged to declare war on Reason. Then I asked myself, well, if consciousness is the thesis and unconsciousness the antithesis, when does the synthesis come about? I think it comes about in the total fusion that is absolute love. That love is different from the everyday article because it implies total honesty, while conventional morality and customs declarations are alike in that both make honest people cheat."

It was that time of the century when black music, black musicians, black dancing, black laughter, were like a fever rising higher and higher every night in the *bôites de nuit* of Paris, and René had been the night before at the *Bal Négre* in Montmartre. Caresse Crosby had taken him there to celebrate the Black Sun Press publication of *Mr. Knife, Miss Fork*, the translation of the first chapter of *Babylon* in a handsome limited edition, illustrated by Max Ernst. And it was of the *Bal Négre* that Rene wanted to speak now.

"The mind of the Frenchman who gets clear of his country," he said, "clear of his conscience and his continence, experiences a liberation. But if for one reason or another he is obliged to remain at home, he demands to be entertained and debauched by the exotic curiosity that lifts him clear of the national fact into an illusion of renewal. Hence the popularity of Martinique jazz, and Cuban melodies, and Harlem bands, and the entire tam-tam of the Colonial Exhibition," he said with bitterness. "Nowadays, the white man regards the man of color precisely as the wealthy Romans of the Late Empire regarded their slaves—as a means of entertainment. And it is no longer necessary, of course, to go to Africa now that our livid capitalism has instituted the prostitution of blacks of either sex. Then, again, the average Frenchman who is not interested in depravities, who is merely seeking the picturesque, can go to the brothel and meet a thoroughbred Negress."

The critic Michel Carassou describes René Crevel as "one of those who are totally committed to the struggle to change life, to the conquest of a new liberty." He speaks of René flinging himself "heart and soul into this adventure, which was also the adventure of surrealism, seeking to tear down all the barriers that set limits to life, that kept the wind from blowing." Carassou says that "the fabulous Africa Crevel recreated" in *Babylon* was "how he had imagined Africa, he who had suffered under every conformity imposed by a bourgeois family who forbade him to go out without socks even in summer at the seashore."

How could he not envy then the " 'Negro' who had not hesitated to toss to the four winds the hypocrisy of jacket and shirt?" Carassou asks, "for it was his own body that Crevel sought to liberate. He wanted to offer his body to every sensation," and then he would be able to say, as he finally did say: "Today my flesh has been freed, and my feet no longer remember socks or shoes." Carassou concludes that in the end the dream remained a dream, and Crevel's surrealism failed to level the walls that separate dream from reality. But René gently, courteously, dismisses this and reminds him in the words of André Breton that the critics have still not understood that "life and death, the real and the imaginary, the past and the future, the communicable and the uncommunicable, the high and the low, will cease one day to be contradictory."

"A world without walls," David reflected. "That's a long way from the Babylon we're living in. The pressures accelerate in your *Babylon*: a gasoline-drinking servant girl, a beautiful cousin with flames springing from her scalp instead of hair, a child who wants to revive the wind of daring and adventure, a rhapsodist of a grandmother spreading her ancient wings in ecstasy. That's quite a cast of characters, and there are more. You are telling us in your *Babylon* that the child, the poet, the dreamer don't live in an enchanted world, but that their eyes alone have the power to see the possibility of enchantment. But when you level the wall between consciousness and language, René, don't you feel at times there's more in the mind than can ever be put into words?"

"David, the least of my words exceeds the sum of all my thoughts," René answered. "This makes me feel alternately joy or shame, not knowing if the butterflies that wing from my mouth are the color of my soul, or if, on the contrary, all my treasures are afloat in the ship of my mind that discipline keeps on course."

It was almost twilight now on the café terrace that we could glimpse from where we sat, and now a few people were beginning to drift into the bar. It would not be long before René would be leaving, and because I was thinking of courage, I mentioned it to him, but I did not speak of his own courage in going to live among strangers. Yet I believe that he knew.

"Just courage in a general sense," I said, and I did not look at him, but at the lights coming on in the avenue outside.

"Well, courage historically," he said, accepting the pretext of generality as if the idea were his own. "A single drop of fear and we have a whole ocean of ferocity. For centuries and centuries, religion was delegated to do the dirty work of repression, restraining the courageous, desensitizing them with menaces, and freezing and paralyzing them by means of terror and assault. . . ." He said that from the very dawn of the French Revolution, the Pope had condemned the Declaration of the Rights of Man. "I mention this," René said, "because today the High Priests of capitalism, like the Holy Fathers of the bloodiest marches in history, exalt murderous generalities."

"And is that what courage is?" I asked.

"Courage or not," he went on, "for Christian masochism there has never been any progress that wasn't a sin. It is the same ones who now exalt courage for the sake of courage, as if a man's courage could have any other purpose than the material or moral amelioration of his existence, as if the actions taken to express that courage should be in opposition to the body, in opposition to the mind, as if the vision of things should be separated from the eye that perceives them, and ideas severed from the brain that thinks them." For a moment his eyes were dark with anger as he said: "There is nothing more macabre than the uniforms in which dictators deck out their mercenaries in the name of courage—black shirts in Italy, shirts the color of intestinal scoria in Germany, skulls on the amulets of the Franco-ists!"

And then, seeking to save us from irreparable despair, he began to laugh.

"But let me tell you the shroud of times already past will never be able to serve as winding-sheet for the star of revolution," he said. "No more than night can prevent the day from dawning, or cold metal keep fire from springing to life when two stones are rubbed one against the other; the change will come. All the blood that has been shed, blood that coagulated to pave the way for the apocalypse of imperialism, will be reabsorbed and will flow over the rubbish of a society in its decline. After so much putrefaction, so many assassinations, the confusion will be cleared away. There will then be born, will come to life, a prism at the same time single and innumerable, and, farther than any horizon or custom, a sun of fire and brimstone will suddenly blaze. And then we shall have a society without classes, without churches, without frontiers. And this is why," he said, speaking triumphantly, yet with a certain shyness and humility, "this is why surrealism has cast its lot with the proletariat, which in liberating man will liberate his mind as well."

It was then that René stood up from the table in the Coupole Bar, the brown paper parcel of the translation of *Babylon* under his arm, not wanting to linger over the farewells. But when he opened his mouth to speak to us, no sound could be heard, no words came. This was because in June 1935 he had taken his own life at the age of thirty-five. Instead it was Anna Balakian who spoke.

« A CONVERSATION »

"René, you have defined poetry as the burning center of the self," she said. "You have achieved the poetic metaphor that studs with stars and warms with sparks your prose, as it does the *Illuminations* of Rimbaud and the *Cantos* of Lautréamont —a perpetual *mise en abyme*, your song of the depths. Oh, René, how mean not to have lived out your life. Oh, René, how mean, how cruel . . ."

(Although the words, the sentences, spoken by the four participants in the "Conversation with René Crevel" were at one time or another spoken or written by them, this meeting in the Coupole Bar could not—if the reader insists on Reality—have taken place.)

K.B., 1984

Design by David Bullen
Typeset in Mergenthaler Granjon,
Bodoni, and Bauer Bodoni
by Wilsted & Taylor
Printed by Maple-Vail
on acid-free paper